W9-BAI-415

MIRANDA

MIRANDA

Vicki Page

Chivers Press • G.K. Hall & Co.
Bath, England Thorndike, Maine USA

This Large Print edition is published by Chivers Press, England, and by G.K. Hall & Co., USA.

Published in 1999 in the U.K. by arrangement with the PDSA.

Published in 1999 in the U.S. by arrangement with Chivers Press Ltd.

U.K. Hardcover ISBN 0–7540–3531–X (Chivers Large Print)
U.K. Softcover ISBN 0–7540–3432–8 (Camden Large Print)
U.S. Softcover ISBN 0–7838–0359–1 (Nightingale Series Edition)

Copyright © Vicki Page 1983

All rights reserved.

The text of this Large Print edition is unabridged.
Other aspects of the book may vary from the original edition.

Set in 16 pt. New Times Roman.

Printed in Great Britain on acid-free paper.

British Library Cataloguing in Publication Data available

Library of Congress Cataloging-in-Publication Data

Page, Vicki.
    Miranda / Vicki Page.
      p.   cm.
    ISBN 0–7838–0359–1 (lg. print : sc : alk. paper)
    1. Large type books.   I. Title.
    [PR6066.A355M57   1999]
    823'.914—dc21   98–33778

CHAPTER ONE

As the road ribboned out ahead and the mileage ticked up on the clock, I felt my inward tension growing. The windscreen wipers moved at a rhythmic pace, forming tiny rivulets of water on the windscreen as the rain sheeted down, obliterating much of the view ahead. I wondered if the foul weather was symbolic of ill-omen but swiftly thrust the unpleasant thought aside.

Now and again I cast a covert, sidelong glance at Gavin as we travelled swiftly along the narrow Cornish lanes towards Herren Towers. His face was set, his gaze firmly fixed on the road in front of us as he concentrated on his driving. I felt excluded from him, as if he had placed an invisible barrier between us. Involuntarily I gave a tiny shiver and, for a brief moment, he lifted a hand from the steering wheel and pressed it firmly over mine in a comforting gesture.

'Nervous, Louise?'

A smile flickered about the sensitive line of his lips and he threw me a glance which contained more than a hint of challenge in its depths.

'What do *you* think?' I countered. 'Wouldn't you be feeling nervous if our situations were reversed?'

1

'If I were a bride as beautiful as you,' he replied, 'I'd be thinking how fortunate the Summers' family should consider themselves to welcome me as an addition.'

I snorted unceremoniously and, as if anxious to drop the subject himself, Gavin did not pursue his arguments. Silence surrounded us once more in the warm interior of the car; it was a silence which pressed in on us giving the impression of an unseen third.

I turned away from Gavin, trying to pierce the rain-swept side-window of the car to watch the passing scenery. The rain and the fast encroaching darkness of this February evening made visibility almost nil; all I could see in the glass was my own reflection, pale and tense.

Beautiful? Gavin thought I was beautiful? I smiled wryly to myself as I studied my face, taking each feature and assessing it with the total impersonality of a stranger.

Brown hair curling under at chin level, widely spaced brown eyes, tilting upwards at the corners with a vaguely Oriental cast about them and fringed with heavy black lashes—my one gift endowed by Nature. High cheekbones and a small, rather determined chin, jutting out at the moment in an expression my father would instantly have recognized as 'Louise's defiant face'. My mouth—too wide to conform to beauty's demands was, at this moment, unsmiling and there was an almost disconsolate droop to its corners. Hurriedly I

2

controlled my expression, forcing myself to look like everybody's idea of the happy bride being taken to meet her new in-laws.

But it was not quite such a simple situation in view of the speed at which our whirlwind romance had blossomed. I could not conceal my inner trepidation as I wondered how Gavin's family were going to react to the arrival in their midst of the second Mrs. Summers.

From the moment that Gavin stepped into the Brownholt Museum in his quest for a particular item of information about Ramses II of the nineteenth dynasty of Pharaohs which he needed for an article he had been commissioned to write for a well-known and erudite journal, I knew that I had handed him my heart as well as the pile of dusty old files and books on the subject. I had worked in the Museum for the past four years, entering employment there as a filing clerk when I was twenty and working my way to the position of assistant curator.

Egyptology had long been my pet subject and the Brownholt Museum had gained a considerable reputation for its fine library of books dealing with many facets of the history of the Pharaohs as well as the excellent collection of artefacts it housed beneath its Victorian roof.

Gavin Summers' name was as familiar to me as my own. His photograph had graced many a

3

newspaper column; in his early thirties, dark-haired and skin tanned by the time he had spent in Egypt, his features were distinctive and prepossessing. Green eyes which held an almost magnetic quality in the level way they regarded one, the long hawk-like nose, the obstinate cleft chin belied by the gentle mouth with its firm lips. His writings on the subject had been a key source of information for any who sought to increase their knowledge on the fascinating and mysterious secrets of the Ancient Egyptians. I had never expected to meet him personally and when David Ross introduced us and told Gavin that 'Miss King is one of the ablest assistants I've ever had', I felt myself positively glow beneath the warmth of praise.

The sharp look which our unexpected visitor gave me, ranging from the tip of my head to the toes of my feet, left me glowing even more; slightly breathless, too, a strange embarrassment taking hold of me as I recognized the frankly admiring expression which gleamed in Gavin's green eyes.

Even so I had not been prepared to find him waiting for me in the car outside the Museum when I left that evening. The cool arrogance and self-assurance which I quickly learned to equate with this man would not allow him to accept the fact that I had already made arrangements to visit a friend in the evening and I was not surprised to hear myself calling

4

Dorothy on the phone to tell her that 'something had come up unexpectedly'.

By the end of that week I knew I had fallen head over heels in love with Gavin. I accepted the fact that it was a foolish, hopeless love which could not possibly have any fulfilment and I resolved to enjoy every hour I could in his company until, his research completed, he returned to his home in Cornwall.

When he asked me to marry him I thought I must surely be dreaming. I heard myself accept his proposal as if the words came from a long way away, as if the voice belonged to somebody else. I was aware only of his arms around me as he swept me into an embrace which I wanted to last for ever.

It was then that I received the first shock.

He told me that he was a widower. Two years previously Miranda, his wife, had been drowned in a boating mishap and the Coroner's Court had brought forward a verdict of 'Death by Misadventure'. Those brief words had brought to an official conclusion four years of marriage.

His words were stark and few. Clearly it caused him pain to remember the past events and I, so full of the happiness he had just bestowed on me with his proposal, begged him not to speak of it any more. It was sufficient that he had told me he loved me . . . sufficient that he wanted me to share his life with him.

We married almost immediately, neither of

us wanting a big wedding with a lot of fuss and publicity. We had a brief honeymoon in Italy which drew us together in an even closer affinity with each other.

It was only now as we travelled towards Herren Towers and I was within such a short time of actually meeting the family who, until now, had been only faceless names to me, that I realized how little I really knew about the man sitting beside me. I stole another glance at his sharply defined profile, feeling the vague sense of apprehension once again touch the nape of my neck with icy fingers. I tried to push the foolish feeling aside but it would not allow itself to be dismissed so easily.

'Tell me about Miranda.' The words shot out with the velocity of a bullet, shattering the thick and heavy silence which enclosed us.

'Now?' Surprise sounded in Gavin's voice and I saw his hands tighten momentarily on the steering-wheel. 'You do pick your moments!' he went on, injecting a lighter note. 'We're within half a mile of Herren Towers now. It's hardly the time or the place to tell you about her. Why the sudden curiosity anyway? You didn't want to pry into my murky past when I tried to talk to you about it before we married.'

'Pry? I'm sorry you take a natural interest as prying.' Gavin's poor choice of words stung me into a sharp retort. I felt myself withdraw even further into the corner of my seat; it was an involuntary gesture but I knew that he had noticed the action and misinterpreted it.

'You're snappy! Are you tired? This damn weather is scarcely calculated to improve the local scenery. Cheer up, Louise. We'll soon be home.'

Even as he was speaking he slowed the car down in front of some large wrought-iron gates; peering through the misty rain I was just able to discern the name 'Herren Towers' picked out in gold against the black tracery. They were closed against us and the fact seemed strangely unwelcoming. I could not shake off the unpleasant sense of presentiment which had dogged all our journey since we had arrived at the airport earlier in the day.

Lowering his head against the incessant rain, Gavin jumped out of the car and, moving with swift, lithe strides towards the gates, he pushed them wide open. As he climbed back into the driving seat I saw that even those few steps had been sufficient to drench him in the torrential downpour. Raindrops pearled his face like sweat and his dark hair was slicked down, shining like black ebony in the dim lighting.

As if he felt me watching him, he turned towards me. The expression on his face was suddenly serious as, without warning, he pulled me into the circle of his arms.

'I love you, Louise. Never doubt it ... never.' His lips were against my own as he whispered the words, an almost savage intensity in the emphasis he gave them. The kiss which followed this statement was hard and fired the thrill through all my body which his touch had never failed to arouse.

Then, almost as abruptly, he released me and switched on the ignition, accelerating the car through the open gates and down the long, tree-lined drive leading to Herren Towers.

The grounds spread out in either direction, filling me with a sense of awe. Gavin had tried to prepare me for the size of the estate which had been in his family for the past four hundred years or more. I knew that the woods to the left led down directly to Herren's Cove where, as a boy, Gavin had learned to swim and sail with his younger brother, Philip. To the right were the meadows and lush green fields where the Home Farm and tenants' cottages were situated although I could see nothing of them as we travelled swiftly along the private driveway leading to the house.

The drive seemed to go on and on. I began to wonder when we should arrive at the house itself. Then, suddenly, there was a sharp turn to the right, and Herren Towers stood before us, square and sturdy, nestling in a valley.

I do not think I shall ever forget my first sight of the grey house which was to be my new home. There was grace and beauty in every aspect of its structure; the architect who had designed it, all those centuries ago, had planned it with love and with minutest attention to detail. It seemed to speak of the generations who had sheltered beneath its roof, the family love which had gathered in the warmth of its security.

Lights shone welcomingly from all the eight mullioned windows on the ground floor, spilling from the open front door over the steps and surrounding terraces in a great pool of glistening silver as it met the rain-drenched stone.

'Here we are. Herren Towers greets its new mistress. Welcome home, darling.'

Gavin's voice broke into my awe-stricken silence as he stopped the car in front of the main entrance. I could find no words to answer him or to express the impression the house had made upon me. I had formed no preconceived ideas as to what I expected to see. I knew only that the reality of Herren Towers far exceeded any image I could have conjured up in my imagination.

Turning towards him, I saw that he was smiling slightly. It was as if, with that unerring instinct he possessed for perceiving my deepest feelings and moods, he guessed that I was bereft of words. Too overwhelmed even to respond to his smiling introduction to this house which was to be my future home.

'Well, Louise, take a deep breath.' Although he spoke lightly, teasingly, there was an underlying warning in his tones. 'You are now about to meet the Summers' ménage.'

'There's no need to remind me,' I said. 'I'm shivering in my shoes at the prospect. Oh, Gavin! Suppose they don't like me?'

'Idiot!' Leaning forward he planted a light kiss on my cheek; his lips felt cold and there was still a dampness on his skin left by the rain. 'They're all going to love you nearly as much as I do.'

I wished I could believe him but, unbidden, I seemed to sense that odd tension mounting once again. I wished that we had arrived in daylight; somehow the fast approach of night was stifling me, filling me with a claustrophobic fear which I could not explain. I wished that I had paid more attention when Gavin had spoken to me about the other members of the family. I wished . . .

I stopped myself. It was useless to waste energy in such a futile way. Wishes would not help me over the hurdle of the next few hours.

CHAPTER TWO

I drew in a deep breath as Gavin opened the car door for me. I summoned up all my courage for the ordeal ahead of me—then chided myself for that word 'ordeal'. Should the introduction to my new family warrant such an extreme description?

10

He took my arm, leading me up the wide stone steps to the entrance. I felt a wild urge to run away but forced myself to smile up into Gavin's face as I felt his eyes watching me, clearly trying to guess my first impression of the imposing entrance hall in which we stood.

It was large and square with a magnificent tiled floor; a log fire crackled welcomingly in the far corner, its bright flames reflecting cheerily in the suit of armour which stood in a nearby niche. A curved staircase led to a long half landing, along the wall panels of which hung a line of portraits. I guessed they must be predecessors of Gavin and resolved to study them at the first opportunity. A refectory table in the middle of the hall contained a large copper jug of daffodils and forsythia; a pleasing reminder of springtime in these unfamiliar surroundings on this cold, wet night.

Gavin helped me off with my coat, signalling with a finger on his lips for silence.

'We'll surprise them,' he murmured in my ear. 'They haven't heard the car or they would have been out to greet us by now.'

Taking my hand he led me to a door at the right of the panelled hall. I was uncomfortably conscious of my damp hair falling in wispy tendrils about my face. I wished that I had had time to change my shoes, too, when, glancing down on the tiled floor, I glimpsed the wet trail of footprints we had left behind us.

11

Gavin opened the door sharply, startling the occupants sitting around the glowing coals of the fire. For a second the faces were turned towards us, surprised and alert. Nobody made a move and, for a long time afterwards, it was as if that small cameo was impressed into my memory. Whenever I recalled my introduction into Herren Towers it was that tiny scene which memory conjured up. That moment of silent appraisal before speech became general and the introductions were being made.

It was Philip who was the first to jump to his feet, advancing towards us with outstretched hand to Gavin and a welcoming, brotherly kiss on the cheek for me.

'So you're the mysterious Louise, are you?' he smiled, standing back to regard me from head to foot. What he saw seemed to satisfy him for he cast a frankly envious glance at Gavin. 'She's a winner, old man! You can certainly pick 'em!'

The words jarred on me faintly and I tried to withdraw my hand from the firm grasp. But Philip would not allow me to escape so easily. He held on tightly, the smile still playing about his lips.

'I don't think there's anything very mysterious about me,' I said lightly.

'There has to be some sort of mystery attached to any woman who has the power to rush my brother into marriage at such breakneck speed.'

I felt a surge of annoyance. He made it sound as if I were a fortune-hunter who had deliberately inveigled Gavin into marriage.

'I wasn't aware that I rushed him into anything,' I retorted. 'If I remember correctly, it was more the other way about.'

Philip's eyes met mine with an imp of mischief dancing in their depths.

'Oh, nothing personal, I assure you, dear sister-in-law. It was just that none of us expected old Gavin to—'

'Look, Philip, do you think you could step aside and allow Louise and myself to come into the room to meet Mother?'

Gavin's voice, crisp and incisive, cut into Philip's sentence with disregard. He seemed not to mind, however, as stepping aside with a gallant gesture of his hand, he apologized for blocking our progress into the room.

He followed a pace or two in the rear of us as Gavin led me towards the tall wing-back armchair nearest the fireplace. I was acutely conscious of Philip's eyes still watching me intently. Despite his winning smile and friendly manner I felt a certain distrust of him. His playboy air and the unveiled admiration in his eyes served to intensify my sense of discomfort in these unfamiliar surroundings and there had been undercurrents in that brief exchange which left me oddly disturbed. I made up my mind to ask Gavin when we were alone exactly why it was that he had surprised his family so

13

much.

But for now the vague uneasiness was forgotten as Gavin introduced me to his mother. White-haired and elegant, Alice Summers' features held a sweetness which warmed me. Suddenly I felt welcome in Herren Towers, recognizing that until this moment a certain disquiet had marred my entry into the house.

'Welcome to Herren Towers, child,' she said, patting the small stool beside her. 'You must be both cold and tired after your journey. Warm yourself at the fire then Gavin shall take you to your room to change for dinner.'

My heart sank slightly. I wished we could have dispensed with the formality of dinner but, clearly, the family had waited for us to arrive so there seemed no courteous way of escape from the meal. Obediently I took the place she indicated, enjoying the warmth of the fire as I held out my cold hands to the glow.

'We'll talk together tomorrow, Louise,' she said softly, 'meanwhile, just let me wish you much happiness with my son. It is good to have a daughter-in-law in residence once again at Herren Towers. Miranda was a tower of strength to us all.'

Even as I warmed my body at the fire, a chill touched my spine. I was made aware once again of the unseen presence of Miranda Summers and, inexplicably, suddenly felt myself resented by these people who had

14

voiced a warm welcome. It was as if their enmity had formed itself into a tangible substance around me. I tried to shake off the impression of an unseen evil in the atmosphere, telling myself that a house as old as this must carry such an aura in its history; love: hatred: jealousy. All must be impregnated in its very timbers.

Before I could respond, Gavin cut in, reminding them that we were both weary after our journey from the airport.

'The weather was atrocious,' he remarked to all and sundry. 'I don't think the rain ceased for a moment as we drove down. We certainly knew we were back in England. By the way, Philip, I bumped into an old friend of yours in Rome ... Rodney Fullerton. Remember you brought him to spend a weekend here last year? He seemed anxious to contact you. Has he phoned at all?'

The change of subject had been deftly made. Miranda's name had caused only a brief hiatus in the conversation. But I was as aware of her physical presence as if she stood beside me in the room. I wondered why Gavin seemed so reluctant to speak about her ... why he should be so eager to dismiss all mention of her as if the years of their marriage had never been.

Was this to be the future pattern of our life here at Herren Towers? Was the ghost of Miranda to stand in the background of all we

15

said and did? Were the family to be silent witnesses to unexpressed comparisons?

I felt a tiny shiver move down my spine. Misunderstanding it, Gavin took my hand and lifted me to my feet.

'Come, Louise! A bath and change of clothing is indicated. You'll feel better for it.'

I allowed myself to be led from the fireside, my gaze slipping away from Philip's frankly over-admiring expression. I found it oddly disconcerting and sensed that Gavin guessed my confusion.

'By the way,' he said, as we crossed the room, 'where's Annabel? I expected her to be here.'

It was Philip who replied, with a casual air: 'She's in town for the night. She'll be back tomorrow, I understand.'

Gavin nodded in silent response as we left the room.

We were just crossing the hall towards the staircase when a little old lady opened the door on the opposite side of the hall. She opened it surreptitiously, inch by inch, and, fascinated, I watched as first one rheumy eye appeared and then the other; the bird-like features of the tiny face were topped by a mass of white hair gathered into an untidy top-knot on the crown of her head. There was a peculiar, elfin charm about the small creature who watched us timidly for a moment before she lifted a wrinkled hand and beckoned to us with a long, bony finger.

I heard Gavin utter a small sound but, so indistinguishable was it, I was unsure whether he laughed or breathed a soft imprecation.

Taking my arm, Gavin led me away from the staircase and towards the diminutive little woman who stood watching us, an expression of eager expectancy on her face.

'Hello, Aunt Hettie!' he smiled. 'Allow me to introduce my wife to you.'

She held both hands out to me and I took them in my own as she nimbly stepped backwards and drew me into the room. Gavin followed close on our heels, closing the door behind him as he did so.

'Your wife, dear? But I've already met her, haven't I?' A vague light lit her eyes as she regarded me closely. Then, the light fading and a disappointed note entering her voice, she continued: 'She's changed. Not as I remember her at all.' She shook her head soulfully, as if she could not account for the vagaries of a memory which escaped her.

'This is Louise, Aunt Hettie,' explained Gavin patiently. 'My wife, Louise. Louise, this is Aunt Hettie. I've spoken of her to you.'

'How do you do?' I said.

I tried to remember what he had told me of this elderly relative. I believed she was actually a great-aunt of Gavin's but the details of the involved relationship escaped me in those moments of introduction. I recalled he had

17

told me that her memory occasionally played tricks on her and she believed herself to be living in the past instead of the present. I had my verification when she turned to Gavin with a chiding smile, her head tilted to one side, resembling an inquisitive sparrow.

'Miranda, you silly boy! Fancy forgetting your wife's name! Oh, how he teases you, my dear.'

'*My* name is Louise,' I said slowly. 'I've—'

'Miranda had an accident, Aunt Hettie. Don't you remember?'

'Accident?' She eyed him vaguely, questioningly. 'Won't you sit down and tell me about it, dear?'

'We're just going up to change for dinner. I'll come and see you tomorrow,' he promised her gently.

'Will you come, too, Miranda?' she asked, turning towards me, entreaty on her features. 'Will you come and take tea here with me?'

I nodded. 'If you would like me to,' I accepted hesitantly.

Glancing around the crowded and old-fashioned room I could see that it was used as a bed-sitting room. It seemed that the family kept Aunt Hettie in here to live out her remaining days and I left a stir of pity for this frail creature who continued to eye me in a puzzled fashion.

'You always used to come for tea and a chat,' she said. 'Do you remember how you

18

enjoyed toasted buns by the fire, Miranda? You haven't been for such a long time. I've missed you.'

'Aunt Hettie, this is Louise—not Miranda.'

Gavin's voice came firmly but he shot me an apologetic glance as he spoke, taking my hand as if to offer me silent reassurance.

The old lady's face crumpled momentarily, reminding me of a child who hesitates on the brink of tears—that crucial moment when it stands poised for an angry outburst against the harshness of fate.

'Where's Miranda?' she asked now, her voice plaintive, shrill. 'Where's Miranda? Why does she never come to see me? *Why*, Gavin? Take *her* away!' She threw me a vicious glance of dislike from those watery eyes. 'Take her away! I don't like her.'

Gently he led her to the armchair beside the fire, his face kind but his expression full of a total weariness which etched the lines more deeply about his eyes and mouth.

'We'll come back and talk tomorrow,' he promised her. 'We'll see you then.'

We left the room together, the silence between us separating us as if it stood in solid, rock-like substance between us. Outside in the hall he turned me to face him, running a tender hand down my cheek in a familiar gesture of affection which, until this moment, had never failed to fill my heart with a sense of warmth and wonder that, from all the world, he should have chosen me to share his life. Now I felt oddly estranged by the touch of his hand; my instinct was to move away as if he were a stranger who dared to take an inexcusable liberty. But I forced myself to stand, unresponsive to the caress. I remembered the closeness we had shared in Italy and compared it with this homecoming.

Aware of my cool apathy he dropped his hand and a closed expression flitted into his eyes. I sensed that he had been on the point of saying something but changed his mind, contenting himself with a brief apology.

'I'm sorry about that, Louise. She *is* very old and very forgetful.'

'It doesn't matter,' I replied, and knew even as I spoke that my calculated air of disinterest had disappointed Gavin. 'As you say, she's old.'

'Another two years and she'll make her centenary,' he went on as we climbed the elegant staircase. 'On her good days she's already started to make plans for the celebrations at Herren Towers. The only trouble is that her guest list contains the names of many of her contemporaries who have long since gone.'

We made conversation as he headed us towards our room. There was a constraint between us which held us together yet apart as he took my hand and drew me into the master room which was to be our bedroom.

Inside the room he shut the door and,

drawing me to him, kissed me with passion. I felt a return of the blood surging through my veins as he held me close. The warmth of his body seemed to restore life to my own.

'We'd better get changed and go down,' he said, after a few minutes. 'The hurdle of the Summers' family at dinner is your next test of endurance. My poor Louise! It can't be easy for you!'

There was compassion in his eyes as he smiled down on me.

'As long as you're there, I'll be able to bear anything,' I said staunchly. 'Even the Summers' family *en masse*—and you *are* a rather awe-inspiring gathering, you know!'

He laughed over his shoulder as he turned towards the bathroom which adjoined this large bedroom.

'Awe-inspiring? I shouldn't have thought that a good adjective to describe us, Louise. Just remember you're the new mistress of this place and keep your chin up. Don't let anybody over-awe *you*, my love.'

He was gone before I could ask him to enlarge on the words which were so clearly intended to remind me of the authority he wished me to wield in Herren Towers. I wanted to ask him why he should think it necessary to adjure me to keep my chin up but the sound of the running bath water drowned all possibility of discussion between us.

I shrugged hopelessly, dismissing the subject

from mind as I looked about me at the unfamiliar surroundings of the room. The thick green carpet and gold furnishings were tasteful and gave an air of comfort in the heavily oak-panelled room; as well as the large bed—a fourposter, I noted with a smile. One almost thought there should be a small plaque stating that Queen Victoria had slept here!— there was an elegant chaise-longue and several comfortable armchairs; a dressing-table; near the window, a writing-desk and small straight-backed chair.

I crossed to the window, my feet sinking into the thick pile of the carpet. Pulling back the heavy gold velvet curtains which somebody had already drawn, I tried to penetrate the darkness of the night to catch a glimpse of the gardens below; all I could discern was the patterning of the rain on the windows and black clumps of bushes and trees which surrounded the grounds. I pressed my forehead against the glass, suddenly filled with an overwhelming sense of depression and feeling unutterably weary. Alone for the first time since this morning I was able at last to drop the air of bravado I had assumed.

It would be foolish to pretend that meeting Gavin's family for the first time had not been something of a test. I found myself wishing that we had married with a little less speed and had paid more attention to the conventionalities; it was only to be expected that the Summers family would resent a stranger's intrusion into their midst. But our love had been too swift, too demanding, to give thought for such considerations.

Lost in my reverie I was surprised by Gavin's arms about me.

'I've run a bath for you, Louise. Better hurry or we'll be late for dinner.'

*   *   *

Reflecting the following day on that meal in the great dining-hall of the house, I admitted to myself that it had not been nearly as intimidating as I had anticipated. The family had set out to put me at my ease and Philip's droll sense of humour had helped to restore my own normal composure. Disappeared now was the taunting manner with which he had greeted me. He set himself out to make an affable impression and I had to admit he succeeded. I considered him far more likeable than my first opinion had given him credit for being.

I was able now to despatch the shadows of apprehension into the back of my mind. The future here at Herren Towers seemed to have slotted into its proper perspective.

After breakfast which was served from seven to nine o'clock in the small room off the main dining-room, I resolved to take a tour of my new home. There had been no time the

23

previous evening and Gavin had arranged to visit the estate manager's office this morning. He told me he would conduct me around the house himself when he returned from going over the accounts with George Fairman, and dealing with any tenants' problems which might have arisen during his absence, but I preferred to go alone. I wanted to take the opportunity to assimilate the atmosphere of this old house where past generations of the Summers' family had been born, lived and died. I felt very aware of the vibrations of those who had impressed their personalities into the walls and rafters of Herren Towers.

My tour was slow and uninterrupted. Aunt Hettie's door remained firmly closed and I had to admit to a certain relief that it had not opened to show her standing there, a bony finger beckoning me in to talk with her.

The house was furnished with charm and style; the private bedrooms on the first floor I did not enter nor did I visit the staff quarters; the portraits on the gallery landing had held me for a long time as I noted the family resemblances which now displayed themselves in Gavin's strong features; the clear-sighted gaze ... the firm mouth and obstinate chin ... The characteristics of his predecessors were firmly etched on his own face.

At last my wandering feet took me back to the long drawing-room where I had met some of the family members the previous evening. It was empty now although a fire crackled merrily in the grate. Vases of daffodils had been placed here and there about the room as if to reassure the world that winter's cold would soon give way to the brighter days of spring. I gave full marks to Mrs. Harkness, the housekeeper, for her discreet care and concern; nothing was out of place about the house and the amount of inconspicuous attention she must give to maintain its perfect appearance was obvious to anybody who looked about them.

Warmed now by the flames as they winged up the chimney, I moved away from the fire and crossed the room to the large writing desk which stood in the corner of the room. Several framed photographs were placed on it and, as I neared the desk, one in particular caught my curious attention.

I picked it up, noting the inscription written in the corner in a bold and flowing hand. It read: *'To Gavin, with love from Miranda'*.

So this was what Miranda had looked like. I studied the large photo with a sinking heart. The long black hair which fell in silky curtains each side of the oval face in its provocative pose; the laughing dark eyes which stared unseeingly up into mine and the full, sensual lips which were curved into a warm and inviting smile.

She was beautiful. The epitome of all men dream about. And once having been married to such a woman, I could not understand what Gavin could ever have seen in me to attract him.

Fascinated I continued to hold the photograph, looking down into it and comparing each of those perfect features with my own ordinary looks.

My pleasure in the day dimmed. Once more the gremlins of my earlier apprehension lurked at the back of my shoulder.

As if in answer to the unspoken thought, a tiny sound came from behind me. Startled, I wheeled around to see who had entered the room with stealthy tread.

I almost dropped the photograph in shock.

For a moment I stood as if atrophied to the spot, unable to accept the evidence of my own eyes.

'Miranda . . .?' I gasped. The name came out as a hoarse whisper. I couldn't control my breathing or the rate at which my heart pounded in the shock of seeing this woman I had believed to have been killed in a drowning accident.

She shook her head, a contemptuous smile lit her face before she extended her hand towards me.

'Hardly!' she murmured. 'I'm Annabel. You must be Louise. Gavin's just been singing your praises to me. Welcome to Herren Towers.' The polite words were not echoed in the cool expression lurking in the depths of her eyes.

26

'Thank you. But—' I broke off, glancing at the photo I still held in my hand, then back at Annabel in question. 'I thought I—' Again I left the sentence unfinished, replacing the frame back on the desk with fingers which shook slightly as I did so.

Annabel's eyes still contained a hint of malicious amusement at my plain discomfiture.

'Apparently Gavin didn't tell you about me?'

I bridled instinctively. 'Naturally he told me that an Annabel Warner lived here as a—a sort of companion to his mother,' I said weakly.

The smile on Annabel's face grew slightly broader, but it did nothing to allay the chill which had entered my bones at the first sight of her standing there.

'But what he apparently didn't make clear to you,' she went on to say, 'was that I'm Miranda's cousin. The resemblance between us is quite striking, isn't it?'

CHAPTER THREE

Heavily wrapped in a sheepskin jacket I walked briskly down the narrow path through the woods in the direction of Herren Cove. The thick trunks of the trees offered protection from the cold east wind which blew with a touch of dampness in the air. I gave an involuntary shiver, huddling closer into the warmth of my coat as the open sea came into view. It looked grey, forbidding. The desolate cry of the gulls overhead seemed to echo around me, emphasizing the fact that I was the solitary occupant of the cove on this dreary morning.

Pausing to look about me at the rock-strewn coast I rested against a tall, monolithic rock; the wind tore through my hair and I pulled a headscarf from my pocket, tying it around my head with difficulty.

Exactly one week had passed since that meeting with Annabel Warner. Polite acceptance of each other now existed between us and I was trying hard to forget the fact that each time Gavin looked at Annabel he must be painfully reminded of his deceased wife. It gave me an uncomfortable awareness of my own deficiencies.

Again and again I found myself wondering what he could have seen in me to make him want to bring me to Herren Towers as his wife. Every time I came in contact with Annabel I was mindful of my plainness and lack of sophistication.

Standing here, back pressed against the rock, I found myself ruminating on the scene which had taken place between Gavin and me after my discovery about Annabel. I had taxed him with my knowledge that night in our room. During the day we were seldom alone long enough to discuss such a private matter.

'Why didn't you tell me that Annabel is your wife's cousin?' I demanded. 'How could you have allowed me to find out so cruelly, Gavin?'

For a moment a touch of softness had entered his eyes, only to be swiftly extinguished as he turned towards me.

'*You're* my wife now, Louise. How many more times do you need telling?'

'As many times as it will take to convince me that you haven't just married me on the rebound.'

His hand shot out, clasping me firmly around the wrist. His fingers bit hard into my flesh but I was almost glad of the pain his grip afforded me—it helped to ease the ache which kept creeping into my heart in spite of all my efforts to keep it at bay.

'Rebound? Why the hell should I marry you on the rebound? I love you. Why can't you accept that, Louise? You seemed to be happy enough when we were on honeymoon.'

'Aren't all newly-weds happy on honeymoon?' I tried to speak lightly but the words came only with difficulty.

'I wouldn't say it was a foregone conclusion,' he returned. 'But you didn't seem to doubt me then. What's happened to change your mind?'

'I—I haven't changed my mind about anything,' I answered miserably. 'It's just that—that—' I broke off, not knowing how to continue, conscious that I sounded merely jealous and spiteful.

He put his arm about me. His closeness filled me with fresh reassurance.

'It's just *what*, my love? Has Philip been getting at you?'

Surprised, I met Gavin's questioning gaze. 'No, of course not. Why should he wish to make trouble for me?'

He disregarded my question and said insistently: 'Then what exactly is worrying you, Louise? I can't put it right unless you tell me.'

'I can't understand why you never said that Annabel and Miranda were related. Why did you leave me to find out like that? I felt so foolish when—when she told me and I had to admit that I didn't know.'

'I'm sorry. Please believe I'm sorry, Louise. I suppose I didn't expect anyone to start chattering to you about Miranda the day after your arrival here.' He paused a moment, lifting my chin and kissing the tip of my nose. His manner was thoughtful as he went on: 'I intended to tell you myself. Of course I should have told you. But somehow, when we were in Italy, I didn't want to break the spell by speaking about a past which contained less than the happiness we were sharing together. Can't you understand that I wanted to wait until you were here at Herren Towers before I told you?'

'I can understand and sympathize with your reluctance to discuss the past with me, Gavin. But I still wish you had prepared me about

Annabel. It was a shock to discover that she was so closely involved with your past.'

'Who told you? Hettie?'

I shook my head. 'No. Annabel.'

His lips tightened into a hard line. 'I should have guessed she'd lose no opportunity in doing so. She idolized Miranda. Nothing she ever did was wrong in Annabel's view. I just thought she might have had a little sympathy for your position here. Being thrown into a lion's den of strangers can't be easy. There was no need for her to be quite so precipitate with her information.'

'Perhaps it wasn't entirely her fault,' I admitted. 'She found me looking at Miranda's photograph—the one you keep on the desk with the other family ones. Naturally, the—' I hesitated, then hurried on—'the resemblance gave me a shock when I turned and saw her standing behind me. She told me then that they were cousins.'

'And, no doubt, enjoyed every moment of telling you.'

His brow was furrowed with lines and I saw tiny marks of strain about his eyes and mouth as he watched me; tell-tale signs which had not been there to see on our honeymoon. Suddenly I longed to turn back the clock to the time we'd spent in Rome together. There had been no shadows then to warn me of the slightly less than happy surprises in store when we returned to Herren Towers.

'Why should she do that?'

For a moment Gavin looked as if he regretted the cynical words, but he made no comment as he bent his head to mine and kissed me firmly.

'Just remember, Mrs. Louise Summers,' he said, lifting his lips for a moment from mine, 'I love you and *you* are the mistress of this house—' he buried his face in my neck and kissed it—'and my heart, Louise.'

Somehow that conversation became lost in the wonder of our lovemaking and neither of us had referred to it again. But now, in the solitude of the grey, wind-swept cove, the ghost of it returned to haunt me, casting its shadows over my heart as I surveyed the wild seas which rushed to meet the shoreline in an excess of white-spumed fury. Desolate and drear. My surroundings matched my mood at that moment.

'Good morning, Mrs. Summers.'

The voice of George Fairman coming from behind, startled me. I turned swiftly, smiling when I saw him standing there, his dark hair blowing wildly as the wind tugged at it. We had met one evening at dinner and I had liked him on sight.

'Taking the sea air?'

'You could say that,' I laughed. 'In abundance, too.'

'I saw you from the top of the cliff. Thought I'd come down and have a word. I don't seem to have seen much of you since your arrival.'

'The weather has hardly been conducive to walking,' I returned. 'I've been learning the layout of Herren Towers. It's somewhat overpowering to the newcomer, you know.'

'I can imagine. Did Gavin give you any idea of the size of the place?'

'None. He merely told me that the estate had been in his family for many years.'

George Fairman cast me a friendly grin, raising his coat collar against the chill, searching wind. There was a comforting ordinariness about his homely features which did much to restore my spirits.

'It must have been quite a surprise. And how do you get on with your new relatives?' Without giving me a chance to reply, he went on: 'Shall we stroll along the beach a little? It's damned cold standing about here. You'll catch a chill.'

Step matching step we moved off from the shelter of the outcrop of rocks and started to make our way along the length of the beach. The wind blew with all its force upon us, making it difficult for us to hear each other speak. Raising his voice against its fury, George Fairman bent his face towards mine, determined to carry on a conversation despite the elements.

'Had you known Gavin long? His news that he was bringing a bride back home with him came as a bit of a surprise to us all.'

'Why? Hadn't you expected him to remarry?' I countered his question with my own.

'Hadn't really thought about it. He seemed immune to feminine charms since—' he hesitated, reluctant to continue.

'Since Miranda's death?' I finished for him.

'Yes.' He smiled down at me, kindly sympathy in his honest eyes. 'Certainly a lot of the local mothers had him lined up for their beloved daughters, but Gavin made it very clear that he wasn't in the running. Yet it seemed that immediately he left Cornwall he fell hook, line and sinker for you.'

'I assure you, Mr. Fairman—'

'Oh, call me George, please!' he cut in. 'We're all very informal hereabouts.'

'Very well. But, as I was saying, I assure you I set no traps for him. Our marriage was just as much of a surprise to my own family.'

'I didn't mean to suggest that you did any such thing.'

'It sounded rather like it to me!'

'It's just that we'd have liked to have been at the wedding, Louise. I suppose I feel swindled out of wedding cake. Were your people present at the ceremony?'

I shook my head. 'My parents are in Brazil at present. My father is a construction engineer and he's engaged in quite a large building project which will take at least a year. My mother went there to be with him. It was a very quiet wedding and, if it's any comfort, nobody had any wedding cake! We didn't bother with it.'

He pulled a wry face and said teasingly: 'Hardly sounds very romantic. I thought all girls wanted flowing white veils and champagne.'

I felt myself beginning to resent the criticism which I sensed in his semi-playful words.

'One shouldn't generalise too much about these matters. Gavin and I chose what *we* wanted.'

'We were pleased to welcome you to the ancestral home anyway,' he said easily.

'Really?' I tried not to allow scepticism to enter my voice but, disguise it how I might, the glance George Fairman shot at me was charged with question.

'You sound a shade doubtful about the welcome.' He grinned. 'Who's been showing their teeth? Annabel?'

'Not so as you'd notice,' I answered. 'But I couldn't help feeling that her reception was rather mixed. I suppose it's understandable. She must consider that I've usurped her cousin's place and resents me for it.'

I marvelled that I found it so easy to confide in this large, amiable man; a bearlike figure hunched into his thick coat and scarf, he gave me just the sense of reassurance I needed at that particular moment. I was speaking to him in the manner I wanted to talk to Gavin but

35

found difficulty in doing. His wall of reserve acted as a barrier between us. George's warm and sympathetic approach was serving to lower the resistance I had built up in self-defence. I felt no sense of disloyalty to my husband. Somehow it was apparent that the estate manager's interest in his employer's business was based only in his sincere friendship for Gavin.

'I suppose so,' he said thoughtfully. 'What about Philip? Met any opposition in that quarter? Has he been getting at you at all?'

I looked at him in surprise that he should have echoed Gavin's own sentiments regarding his younger brother. Why should everybody take it for granted that Philip's acceptance of my presence should be less than cordial?

'Of course not. Should he have done?' There was indignation in my tones but I did not make any attempt to conceal it.

George shrugged. 'He could possibly resent any children which might ensue from your marriage. In the absence of an heir, the estates will pass to him on Gavin's demise.'

I felt a cold shiver touch my spine. 'Oh, don't let's talk about such doleful topics!' I begged hurriedly. 'I'm sure the question of his inheritance isn't uppermost in Philip's mind. As a matter of fact,' I added defiantly, 'I should say he has made me feel more welcome to Herren Towers than anyone else.'

He paused briefly, his arm going around me

in an involuntary gesture of friendship.

'Perhaps I haven't made my own pleasure in your arrival clear,' he said warmly. 'You're exactly what Gavin has needed. You have youth ... beauty ... everything on your side, Louise. Be happy! If there's anything that troubles ... disturbs you at any time, well, I hope you'll tell me about it and allow me to help you.'

'But—*should* anything be going to trouble or disturb me?' Perplexed by his seemingly incongruous remark, I looked up at him questioningly.

'No, of course not.' He appeared to be distinctly uncomfortable for a moment, then he went on swiftly: 'I just mean that should you ever need a friendly ear, you know where to find it. Just knock on good old George's front door!' he laughed.

The strange moment of tension dispersed in the joking words.

'I don't actually know where to find good old George's front door!' I said.

'Oh, I shack up in Myrtle Cottage ... near the Lodge gates,' he offered easily. 'You can't miss it. You'll always be welcome and, if I'm not there, Mrs. Pentravers, my housekeeper, will know when I'll be back.'

'Thanks!' I acknowledged, privately deciding that I should be unlikely to start making social calls on my husband's estate manager.

We walked on a little further together and our talk turned to the theatre and books. Immediately George learned my favourite author was Thomas Hardy his face came alive with enthusiasm.

'I've all his work in pride of place in the cottage,' he said, 'so, if you ever want anything of his, you're welcome to come and help yourself. And now,' he went on, 'if you're going to continue your stroll, I'd better leave you here. I've arranged to call on one of the tenants who has a problem with a leaking roof.'

'Poor tenant!' I commiserated. 'I think I'll go back now anyway. It's really rather chilly. The prospect of the fire and a cup of coffee seems more inviting than all this invigorating fresh air!'

'Your best way back would be to take the path from this cove and follow the road through to the drive gates.' He pointed the direction as he spoke. 'It's an easier route than the way you came by . . . through the woods.'

He touched his cap lightly and was gone, leaving me wondering how he knew that I had approached the cove through the woods. Had he seen me and followed me? . . . paused to chat as if our paths had crossed by sheer accident? I was left with the lingering suspicion that our meeting had not been the chance affair I had at first believed it to be.

CHAPTER FOUR

The idea niggled, preoccupying all my thoughts as I made my way back to Herren Towers, following the directions George had recommended. He was right. I arrived back at the house in less than half the time it had taken me to get down to the cove, but he had omitted to mention that much of the scenic beauty was lost on that more mundane route.

When I arrived back in the house I took off my thick jacket and hung it in the downstairs lobby, then I made my way to the morning room where Gavin had told me he intended to deal with some correspondence. I hoped that by this time he would have finished it and would have time to spare for me.

When I opened the door I was surprised to see Annabel sitting beside the fire. Gavin was in the sofa opposite, his long legs stretched out to the blazing logs and his pose one of indolent pleasure. He smiled when he saw me, patting the vacant space beside him.

'Come here, my energetic little wife. You're just in time for some reviving coffee after your strenuous walk.'

'I'd rather hoped I might be,' I said, as I took the place he indicated.

The fire's warmth was welcome after the chill winds on the beach. I luxuriated in its glow, stretching to receive its comfort like a contented cat. Gavin reached forward, drawing me into the circle of his arm. I felt secure and at ease, resting with my head on his shoulder.

Annabel was pouring out the coffee from a large pot. She handed me a cup, smiling pleasantly.

'There we are, Louise. Gavin was just telling me that he found you in a museum.'

I laughed. 'Yes, but perhaps your choice of wording could be improved on. I worked for the Brownholt Museum, specializing in the Egyptology section. Gavin came there to do some research and—'

'Lost my heart in the process!' he broke in, with a laugh. 'You'd hardly believe such an exquisite creature as this could be so knowledgeable about the Pharaohs, would you, Annabel? Beauty and brains ... how seldom the two are found together.'

'What a chauvinistic remark!' I said, laughing in spite of the swift spurt of irritation which had fired into life at his words. 'And extremely patronizing to boot!'

Annabel joined in the laughter. Then: 'I thought *you'd* found it before, Gavin,' she said. 'You shouldn't be so surprised to find the two qualities are concomitant.'

The subtle reminder of Miranda served to come between us once again, as if a mist had crossed the sun. I felt rather than saw Gavin's withdrawal into himself and, under the pretext of sipping my coffee, I removed myself from

40

his arm. I saw Annabel smile slightly at my discomfiture and eager to ease the sense of strain which had developed, I searched swiftly for a subject of conversation, however trite.

'The seas seemed particularly ferocious today,' I remarked. 'I can't say I'd fancy going out in your boat, Gavin.' He had already mentioned the sailing dinghy which he kept moored in the boathouse in Herren Cove.

He turned to face me, his eyes cold and hard.

'Don't you ever dare to go out unless you're with me, Louise, no matter how fair the weather. Is that clear?'

Surprised by the unexpected intensity of his voice, I nodded. I have never been particularly fond of sailing at the best of times so the stricture caused me no heartburning sense of disappointment. It did, though, cause me curiosity. I decided to ask Gavin later—when we were alone—why he should hold so poor an opinion of my sailing prowess when we had never even discussed the sport! Then I felt myself colour in embarrassment, wishing I could retract my foolish remark about the boat. How could I have been so tactless as to forget that this was how Miranda had met her untimely end! How cruelly my thoughtless words must have hurt both Gavin and Annabel!

Looking up I caught Annabel's speculative gaze on my face. I smiled at her as if seeking

41

understanding and, after an infinitesimal pause, she returned it—but it was tinged with a taunting quality I could not understand.

'But you enjoyed your walk this morning, Louise?'

The question was barbed; her tone contained an inference I could not understand.

'Yes,' I answered. 'I did actually.'

'You followed the woodland path down to the cove, didn't you? It's by far the longer route.'

I wondered how she knew which way I'd walked. It seemed more people than I had guessed had shown an undue interest in my actions this morning.

'So I discovered. I came back the other way. Still, it was more sheltered from the wind. It must be very picturesque in the summer.'

'Indeed it is. But not so quiet as it is now. No matter how many private property notices one puts up to deter the tourists, plenty still manage to make their way to the cove and it's nothing to find large picnic parties in progress down there.'

'I fail to see that it matters,' broke in Gavin, with a laugh. 'There's plenty of room on the beach for a few tourists and us, isn't there? Let's share the amenities we're fortunate enough to enjoy fifty-two weeks of the year without grudging them to those who have only two or three weeks in the vicinity.'

'I dislike seeing litter on the beach,' she said

42

firmly. 'Empty cigarette cartons and plastic food containers fail to fill me with enthusiasm for the members of the public who leave them behind.'

'Be fair, Annabel. In the main, our uninvited visitors leave the place in exactly the condition it's in when they arrive. You just like to have the cove to yourself.'

'I'm sure Louise will feel that way, too,' she said amiably, transferring her attention back to me. She added meaningfully: 'Won't you, Louise?'

I shrugged, puzzled by her question. 'I don't think it will cause me any serious loss of sleep,' I answered lightly, 'if a few visitors want to picnic there.'

'You must admit that onlookers might have cramped your style somewhat this morning.'

She threw me a smile. I sensed animosity despite the teasing friendliness of her tone.

'Meaning what exactly?' I asked.

'Oh, a little bird told me you'd been meeting George Fairman down there this morning.'

She made it sound as if the meeting between George and me had been prearranged. I determined to have no misunderstanding about it. I knew that Gavin was watching my face to assess my reaction to her pointed remark.

'I take it the little bird must have been yourself since you knew I'd taken the woodland path to the cove. But I'd like to make it clear, Annabel, that George just chanced to come down to the cove at the same time. You make it sound as if we had a secret assignation.'

She laughed. 'You seemed to be waiting for somebody when I saw you. Then, after a few minutes, George came down the cliff path towards you and—'

'We strolled along the beach together,' I finished hotly. 'Good heavens, Annabel, I can't think what Gavin must be thinking from the way you speak about such a trivial incident.'

He pulled me to him and gave my cheek a paternal kiss.

'Gavin thinks you're both making a mountain out of a molehill,' he said, playfully. 'George is quite human, after all . . . I couldn't blame him for wanting to spend a few minutes in my wife's company.'

'But it was only a chance meeting,' I tried to emphasize.

'Even if it wasn't, I know I could trust you,' he said—somewhat smugly, in my opinion.

'But George? Could you trust George?' demanded Annabel. Although she spoke lightly the words contained more than a hint of malice. The sharp look she gave me was spiked with interest.

I cast her a reproachful glance. She had been responsible for causing an unpleasant atmosphere around us. Although Gavin had spoken easily, appearing to take little notice of the portents of her words, I knew him well enough to be aware that her veiled innuendo had found its mark. Next time we were all together I should be uncomfortably conscious of George Fairman's friendly attentions; my discomfiture would reveal itself in an embarrassed manner and then Gavin would wonder why his estate manager had the ability to put me out of countenance. Oh, dear! It really was *too* bad of Annabel to stir up a situation where none existed.

'What a stupid thing to say!' I burst out. 'I'm sure Gavin must be well aware he can trust George with his life.'

'Sorry, Louise!' Annabel's apology carried no sincerity. 'I must have been mistaken, of course. It was just that you were leaning on the mermaid rock and I thought you were waiting for him when I saw George appear in the cove.'

'Well, it just shows how wrong one can be in jumping to conclusions because of circumstantial evidence, doesn't it?' I rose to my feet, replacing the cup and saucer on the coffee tray. 'If you'll both excuse me, I'm going to go and do my hair. I feel a mess.'

Before either of them could stop me, I hurried from the room. My heart was beating swiftly and my cheeks burned with the anger I had fought to suppress. Somehow the last few minutes had clouded the morning for me. I found myself regretting the decision to go for a walk at all and then a fresh burst of resentment added fuel to my anger. Why should I be made to feel guilty over such an innocent act?

I paused in the centre of the large hall, trying to regain control over my breathing. I felt as if I had been running and my heart pounded too fast for comfort. It was silly to allow Annabel's troublemaking technique to have such a devastating effect on me, I told myself. But, nevertheless, her words had been designed to plant seeds of doubt in Gavin's mind and the fact angered me.

Even as I stood there, allowing the peace of the empty hall to wash over my unquiet spirit, I heard Aunt Hettie's door open. I glanced in her direction and, as I did so, I saw her thin, white face peer around it before, slowly, she moved forward and her frail form stood revealed on the threshold of her room.

With a sinking heart I watched as she beckoned a scrawny finger in my direction. I was unwilling to be subjected to more of her plaintive demands for me to send Miranda to see her, but I could not ignore the old lady's signal. Forcing a smile I went towards her.

'Louise? Is that Louise?' she demanded, peering short-sightedly at me as she spoke.

My heart leapt in surprise. This was the first time she had appeared to recognize me and call me by name. Things were looking up!

'Yes, Aunt Hettie.' I had fallen into the family habit of addressing her as Aunt Hettie

46

as she appeared to prefer it. 'Can I do something for you?'

'Come and talk to me,' she said. 'I get lonely in my room sometimes now that—'

She broke off but I guessed what she had been about to say—'now that Miranda doesn't come any more'. I sighed wearily and followed her at a creeping snail's pace into the room, helping her to make herself comfortable in her chair in front of the coal fire.

'And how are you settling into Herren Towers, Louise? Adapting yourself to the life here?'

The old lady was remarkably coherent today after the cloudy no-man's land she had seemed to inhabit at all our former meetings.

'Yes, thank you,' I answered. 'It still seems rather big and imposing to me but I suppose I shall become accustomed to its size in time.'

'And Annabel? You get on well with her?' She shot the question out and then cackled with laughter.

'Of course. Should I not?' I remembered the recent scorching encounter but decided that, for diplomacy's sake, I must try to forget it.

'Poor girl! She must resent you bitterly.' There was genuine sympathy in her tone.

'But she must realize that, sooner or later, she would have had to face Gavin's remarriage. If it hadn't been me it would have been somebody else.'

'But she had another candidate in mind for

the post.' Again there issued that eerie, eldritch cackle.

'What do you mean?'

'Isn't it obvious?' Her voice was rising, a shrill note entering it.

'Not to me.'

'She wanted Gavin for herself. And if he hadn't wanted an heir for Herren Towers so much perhaps she would have had her wish.'

I felt my blood running cold. I wanted to escape out of this room and away from this evil old woman with her snide innuendoes. I glanced pointedly at my wrist-watch and made a move to go, not responding to her last remark. But I was not to be allowed to get away so easily.

'Miranda couldn't give him the son he desperately wanted, you see.' She paused, staring into the fire as if the leaping flames were living symbols of the past and the memories she was dredging up from some deep well of the unconscious mind. 'He wouldn't risk such a failure again with her cousin, fearing the same family strain would be present. *That's* why he married *you*, Louise! He wants the son that a fine, healthy girl like you will be sure to give him. But you needn't think he had any other reason for marrying you.'

I started to rush from the room. Her voice followed me, the shrill note had become a screech, reminding me of the cry of a wounded

48

wild creature. I pulled at the door, thankful that it opened and I could feel the colder, fresher air of the hall meeting me as if it welcomed me back into the world of the living, away from the stagnant, closed in atmosphere which surrounded the old lady.

'He loved Miranda... We all loved Miranda...' Her voice cracked, a wailing anguish entered it and, even as I ran across the hall and started to ascend the staircase, I could still hear her calling after my retreating back: 'He doesn't love you. He still loves his wife... Oh, where are you, Miranda? Why don't you ever come to see old Hettie like you used to?'

CHAPTER FIVE

I tried to erase the memory of that scene from my mind. But against my will, it returned over and over to haunt the sleepless hours of the nights and many of my solitary walks down to the cove. The snows of February gave way to the rough winds of March but, instead of time helping me to settle into my new surroundings, it seemed that it was serving only to set me further apart from Gavin.

Somehow I could not understand how or why this gulf should have formed between us. When I remembered the closeness of the days and nights we had shared in Italy... the warm

49

intimacy of those early days of our marriage . . .
I found it difficult to believe that we were the
same two people who had entered into a union
together.

Then I faced the fact honestly. It was I who
was responsible for any division. I was haunted
by the memory of the unknown Miranda.

Although I was now virtually mistress of
Herren Towers, her imprint was to be seen on
everything around me. Even the most minor
change I suggested making usually received
'Oh, Miranda always—' One morning I moved
the flowers on the hall table to a position
where I thought they would be displayed to
better advantage. Half an hour later Annabel
told me: 'I moved the flowers back from where
you put them. We always keep them on the
table. Miranda preferred them there.' A few
days after this incident I mentioned a colour
change in the morning room curtains but my
suggestion was received with chilly lack of
enthusiasm. 'Miranda chose the red velvet
there,' I was informed by Annabel. 'She said it
made the room seem warmer.'

My natural instinct was to point out that I
was now Gavin's wife but I bit back the sharp
rejoinder. Poor Annabel! I could not entirely
stem the pity I felt for her despite not
particularly liking her. She had so clearly been
fond of her cousin that I could understand her
resentment. But each rebuff I received at
Herren Towers served to add another brick to

the invisible wall which separated me from Gavin.

Doubts as to the wisdom of marrying him occasionally struck. I fought them back with determined resistance. I loved Gavin and he loved me. Therefore nothing could mar the relationship between us.

But did he love me?

The insidious question, posed after Hettie Summers' spiteful declaration that he had only married me in order to beget an heir, kept coming back to taunt me with the aggravation of an old sore.

Alice Summers had accepted me with open-hearted warmth after the first few days; but even in her company I felt on guard, ever vigilant for the comparisons I felt sure she must be silently making.

I wanted to tell Gavin all this. I guessed, though, that he would merely tell me I was allowing my imagination to run riot. I preferred to keep my own counsel and when he asked me why I seemed to avoid Aunt Hettie if I could, I made an excuse that I had wearied of being confused with Miranda.

'But she's an old lady, Louise. She means no harm!'

The expression on his face was reproachful, surprised; almost as if he had not expected such unreasonable behaviour from me. I shrugged and the light in his eyes hardened, frozen and turned to ice by my lack of response.

The distance between us increased a little more.

He took me round to meet the farm employees and their families one day. I was keenly aware of the curious eyes which stared assessingly back into mine openly comparing me with the former Mrs. Gavin Summers. I knew that he was increasingly preoccupied with estate problems after his absence from Herren Towers on our honeymoon. He was spending more and more time in the estate office.

I tried to busy myself making plans for the changes I should like to make in the house but I would do nothing until I had had the opportunity of discussing them with Gavin. I wrote letters to old friends and became almost unreasonably pleased when I received a long screed from David Ross telling me how much he missed me at the Brownholt Museum. I even felt a pang of wistfulness when he wrote that my office at the museum would be waiting for me whenever I cared to return.

Somehow when I read those words I suddenly remembered the anxious expression I'd caught in his eyes when Gavin had told him we were to be married; the swift look so promptly dispelled when he had sensed my own regard on him. I wondered why he had felt the doubts he had not voiced aloud in that moment.

I thrust the tormenting thoughts aside, trying to forget my imaginary problems and anxieties.

I encountered George Fairman on several occasions and, with easy friendliness, he would fall into step beside me and escort me on many of my expeditions about the environs of Herren Towers. It was from George that I learned much of the history of the Summers' family, listening with rapt attention as he told me the many legends which had become attached to the splendid old house.

But if his name chanced to come up during any family occasion, I noticed that an air of silent disapproval seemed to hang in the atmosphere about us; however, I was determined not to allow the family's condemnation to mar the friendship which had sprung into being between George and me. It was a pleasant companionship which pleased me after the censorious influence which I so frequently met within the four wall of Herren Towers.

I was constantly aware of the resentment which abounded because I had usurped Miranda's position of mistress in this household. I stepped softly in order not to aggravate the situation—and then chided myself for allowing them—and by 'them' I meant Aunt Hettie and Annabel—to intimidate me, stamping my normal spirit into non-existence.

It was from one of these such walks I returned one day to collide with Alice Summers at the entrance of the driveway. She exchanged greetings with George and stood aside, waiting for me so that we might return to the house together. There was a strain in her manner and the glance she threw at George was vaguely questioning as he called a cheery farewell to me before making his way across the fields in the direction of the estate office.

My mother-in-law and I strode briskly along the tree-fringed drive for a few minutes. The fur coat she wore had a large collar which she held up, framing her white hair, elegantly coiffeured as always; the cold air on her cheeks had brought a bright touch of colour to them, flattering her delicate complexion.

'You seem to meet George Fairman quite frequently on your walks,' she said, her tone expressionless. 'You must be very careful not to give the tenants' food for speculation, Louise. It would not be fair to Gavin for his wife to provide the villagers with a subject for idle gossip.'

I felt myself colour hotly as rage suffused me; then I realized that even my childish habit of blushing so easily might give rise to further conjecturing amongst the Summers family.

'What exactly are you suggesting, Alice?'

She had asked me to call her by her Christian name soon after our first meeting. I think she guessed that I would have found it totally impossible to address her as 'Mother'—a less maternal figure it would have been difficult to imagine—and 'Mrs. Summers' seemed to build a barrier of excessive formality between us.

'I'm hardly "suggesting" anything, my dear, other than that you should be a trifle more circumspect in your dealings with the estate manager. You know how narrow-minded such a small community of tenants and villagers can be.'

'It seems to me that it is not entirely the tenants and villagers who appear to be narrow-minded,' I returned sharply. 'But I hadn't expected that I should have to explain myself to *you*. If Gavin has anything to say about my conduct then I will discuss it with him. Until and *if* that time arises, then I should appreciate it if we could drop the subject.'

'Very well, Louise,' she said, her voice indifferent, shrugging slightly as she spoke. 'I'm sorry that you should resent my advice. It was simply that I wished to help you avoid a rep—' She broke off abruptly, clamping her lips tightly on the words she had been about to speak.

'A repetition, were you going to say?' I demanded sharply.

She regarded me with a cool lack of interest. 'No matter,' she said, after a moment. 'I'm sorry you mistook a friendly desire to help with

55

interference, my dear. You must understand that it has not been easy for us to accept a stranger into Miranda's place in this house. Your marriage was such a hasty affair and a surprise to us all.'

'I should have thought it obvious that sooner or later Gavin would bring somebody to Herren Towers as his wife,' I said coldly.

She gave me a glance which clearly showed me that later would have been preferable to sooner.

We were almost back at the house now and, as if by mutual agreement, conversation ceased between us. We went up the steps in silence and I stood aside to allow Alice to precede me into the hall. There was a strangely dreamlike quality about the simple act of entering the house; it was as if I stood outside myself, viewing my actions and feelings with the disinterested impartiality of a stranger. I was acutely aware in that moment of the sense of discomfort which had developed around me since my introduction into the household; far from being dispelled with a growing familiarity with the Summers' ménage it had intensified with the passing of the days.

Aunt Hettie? A trifle mad perhaps, but nonetheless her undisputed affection for Miranda made it impossible for her to accept another woman in her place.

Annabel? Bitter and resentful in her belief that I had usurped her cousin's position in

Herren Towers.

Alice? Clearly she had been fond of her daughter-in-law and I could not entirely dispel the notion that she regarded me as the unknown quantity. I wondered if she felt uncertainty as to her own future position in the house.

And finally Gavin himself? Ah, now *here* was the unknown quantity as far as *I* was concerned. Secretive. Silent. Deep. A man who did not show his feelings easily but in whom dark passions dwelt beneath the cool surface he displayed to the world. His was not an easy character to know but I had believed I was coming to understand him before we came to Herren Towers. Now I was not so confident and my lack of assurance displayed itself in the wall of reserve which I had unwittingly built around myself.

As we stepped inside the house, Gavin walked out of the library, smiling as he greeted us, his hand outstretched welcomingly towards me. His gaze moved rapidly from my face to his mother's. Curiosity flitted across his features and I knew that, as he assisted us off with our coats, he sensed undertones of the sharp exchange which had just taken place.

Alice cast me a warm, bright smile. 'Shall we have some coffee, Louise?' she asked. 'It might help to drive the chill from our bones.'

I guessed that she wanted to allay Gavin's speculations and, anxious myself to avoid any awkward questions from my husband, I returned her smile as if there were nothing amiss.

'I'll go and prepare it,' I volunteered. 'I expect Mrs. Harkness is busy. You warm yourself beside the fire. I'll not be long.'

Graciously she nodded and, taking Gavin's arm in a possessive gesture, she led him back in the direction of the library.

'Come, Gavin! Talk to me while Louise is busy. I seem to see so little of you nowadays. Poor Louise must think you're wedded to the estate rather than to her. Such neglect is inexcusable. No wonder she has to take so many walks to keep herself occupied while you're out.'

'Poor Louise' made her way to the kitchen fulminating angrily. Alice had made it sound as if I had been grumbling about being bored. I had never resented Gavin's interest in the numerous problems which were entailed in running an estate the size of Herren Towers with all the surrounding properties. I hoped he had the sense to know that I was not so petty-minded nor so incapable of keeping myself amused that I expected him to pay constant attendance on me throughout the day.

Then, deliberately, I stifled the quick surge of annoyance. Alice meant no harm, I told myself. I was being over-sensitive, reading a meaning into her words that she did not intend.

The days moved on in their pattern and the rough and blustering winds of March gave way to an April full of promise. Daffodils, heralding the approach of Easter, danced gracefully in the gardens and the spinney in the wood which led to the cove. I took a fresh enjoyment now in making various minor expeditions on foot about the near environs of the Herren property.

It was on one of these walks that I heard a car slow down behind me. Turning, I saw George Fairman drawing up, a smile on his lips as he poked his head through the open window.

"Morning, Louise. I'm on my way into town. Would you like a lift? Have a coffee with me and then I'll drop you back at the house?'

The spring sunshine made me suddenly restless and, abandoning all sense of discretion, I hesitated only a moment before impulsively accepting the invitation; it was an opportunity for a change of scenery. After all, I could always take my solitary walks but I did not always have the chance of a companion or of visiting the nearby small market town.

Our conversation as we shared the enjoyable morning was innocuous. We spoke of only the most general matters and it was as if we both studiously avoided any mention of Herren Towers or those who lived beneath the shelter of its gabled roof. I felt as if I had been released from the invisible bars of an unseen

59

prison as I revelled in the strange sense of freedom which encompassed me for that brief while.

It was only as we neared the wrought-iron gates that I realized how oppressive the atmosphere of the house had gradually become; the strained manner in which we all treated each other had impinged itself subconsciously upon me and I was suddenly reluctant to return to the stringent politeness which dominated all our attempts at communication. I felt the easy laughter fading from my lips and, unwilling to enter the house too quickly, I hurriedly asked George to drop me off at the gates.

'Stop here, George. I'd prefer to walk back through the woods,' I said. 'It's been a lovely morning. I've enjoyed every minute of it but I'll miss my stroll if I don't take it now. I'm supposed to be doing some typing for Gavin this afternoon.'

He accepted my explanation without argument and drew the large car to a halt.

'We'll do it again some time, Louise,' he said easily. 'Now the better weather is coming I frequently take the car and go off in my free time. It's good to get away from Herren Towers with all its worries occasionally.'

Not waiting for any comment from me, he waved his hand in a swift farewell and drove off down the lane leading to his own cottage. I watched his car move into the distance before I turned and made my way back to the house.

*   *   *

Gavin was preoccupied with the article he was engaged on writing; he displayed no interest in my morning other than to bestow a brief kiss on my cheek and ask mechanically: 'Had a good walk, darling?'

'I didn't have a walk actually. I met—'

Without waiting for an answer to his question he thrust the pile of notes into my hand. 'Louise, what do you think of the phrasing in this paragraph? Do you think a layman would follow the point I'm trying to make?' He went on to discuss the particular point of Egyptian history which he felt needed clarification. 'I'll ring the Brownholt this afternoon,' he said. 'Want me to give David Ross any message?'

His eyes were sharp as he watched my face. It occurred to me that even Gavin was unsure of the situation which had sprung up between us. He was eager to read my reaction to his innocent seeming question.

'Only to thank him for his letter and tell him I'll be writing to him.' I passed the papers back to him. 'This all looks all right to me.'

Satisfied, he nodded and went back to his study. I realized then that I had not told him about my morning excursion with George Fairman. It suddenly seemed insignificant.

I decided not to mention it. It had been a harmless diversion of no importance and perhaps it was better not to risk anyone reading more into it than the matter warranted.

Mentally shrugging my shoulders I went upstairs to tidy my hair before joining the family for luncheon.

CHAPTER SIX

Throughout the afternoon Gavin and I worked together compiling his notes into order. Typing his mass of information I realized once again how meticulous he was about any project with which he was dealing; the minute attention to detail manifested itself over and over again in the papers in front of me.

Once Annabel put her head around the door but, seeing that we were both engrossed with our allotted tasks, withdrew herself and closed the door with an almost ostentatious care, anxious that no slightest noise should divert us from our occupation. I smiled to myself as I remembered the numerous interruptions which had formed part of my daily routine when working for David Ross. I had long ago learned to concentrate on the matter in hand, scarcely noticing the distractions let alone allowing them to interfere with my train of thought.

It was nearly six o'clock when Gavin threw down his pen with a sigh of relief.

'Finished!' he announced triumphantly. 'That's my part completed, Louise. Thanks to you.'

'I've done nothing,' I demurred, 'only something any typing agency would have done equally satisfactorily anyway.'

He stretched out a hand to me.

'My modest, self-effacing Louise! I wasn't really talking about the typing. Just having you with me . . . beside me . . .' He broke off, then: 'Heavens! I'm getting sentimental! Let's go and change for dinner before I start telling you I love you or something equally romantic.'

I laughed. 'I've a better idea! Let's not bother about dinner but—'

He caught me in his arms, kissing me with a sudden hunger which caught me off guard. I responded with equal passion and it was only the sound of Alice Summers talking to Mrs. Harkness in the hall that brought us back to the reality of the present moment. He released me from his embrace and, hand in hand, we made our way upstairs to our bedroom to change for dinner.

'Wear that white thing with the blue belt,' demanded Gavin. 'I like that.'

'White *thing* indeed!' I remonstrated playfully. 'Let me tell you that white thing set me back nearly a month's salary cheque. You should at least speak of it with respect.'

Somehow the atmosphere between us had lightened into the happier one which had existed before we came to Herren Towers. I felt the shadows of care receding from me as we came together in the glow of warm affection which brought us into a close affinity of spirit. I loved. I felt loved. Once more I asked myself what more I could ask from life than this union with a man whom I respected above all others.

Dinner was almost over when Annabel sprang her surprise. There had been a complacent air about her, the self-satisfied manner of one who is well-pleased with herself.

'I came in while you were working this afternoon. Neither of you noticed me. You were too busy.'

'What did you want, Annabel?' asked Gavin. 'You know I don't care for interruptions when I'm concentrating.'

'Oh, we all know the house could fall down around you while you're working and you wouldn't care one jot, but it was Louise I actually wanted to talk to.'

'Why?' I asked.

Gavin looked up sharply, his gaze flicked from Annabel's face to mine and back again.

She hesitated a moment as if carefully figuring out her words. 'There was a letter for you, dear—it was delivered by hand together with ... this.' From her pocket she drew a small tissue-wrapped paper and a note, handing them to me across the table. 'I opened the envelope after I left you both working as it worried me. I wondered how urgent it was and if I could help.'

How dare she open my correspondence! I felt annoyance rising within me, consuming me and suddenly destroying my earlier sense of well-being.

I opened the small packet and, to my surprise, a narrow gold chain bracelet identical to the one I wore fell from it. I looked swiftly at my wrist, and saw that my own was missing from my arm and I had not noticed its absence. Even before I read the brief handwritten note which accompanied it, I guessed what it would contain. But before I could unfold the note Gavin took it from my hand and started to read aloud:

'*"Dear Louise"*—' he read, glancing up at me—'*"You left this behind in the car this morning. I didn't want you to be anxious about having lost it so decided to send one of the farmhands up to the house with it. Thanks for giving me your company. Let's do it again some time—very soon!"*'

Gavin's voice was cold as he added: 'It's signed *"George".*'

65

He looked up, meeting my eyes levelly. I tried to speak but no words would come.

'You didn't say you'd been with Fairman this morning,' he went on, his tone accusing. 'Why the big secret, Louise?'

'I tried to tell you when I came back,' I answered defensively, 'but you weren't listening to me.'

He cast me a disbelieving glance. 'And have I not been listening to you ever since?' he demanded quietly.

'We—we've been busy,' I replied, aware that my explanation sounded weak, a contrived excuse to account for the fact that I had been caught out in an act of deceit. I heard Annabel give a soft laugh and rounded sharply on her. 'And as for you, Annabel,' I stated angrily, 'I should appreciate it if you would kindly refrain from opening correspondence addressed to me in future.'

'Certainly, Louise,' she said, falsely contrite. 'You really must forgive me, dear. I didn't realize you were hiding secrets from Gavin. It was foolish of me to believe you would *surely* have told him that you'd been out with the estate manager this morning. I didn't dream you hadn't mentioned it . . .'

Without a word Gavin rose from his seat at the table and started to walk towards the door.

'Gavin? What about coffee?' I asked.

He paused, regarding me with the impersonality of a stranger. Then: 'Coffee?' he repeated, before sharply adding: 'No, thanks. I'm going to check a few estate figures in the study. Don't wait up for me, Louise. I'll be late.'

CHAPTER SEVEN

I do not remember the rest of the events of that evening. I marked it only as the dividing line which separated the two phases of my marriage. Between Gavin and me there was a sense of strain; it was as if there were matters which should be brought out into the open and discussed but neither of us was willing to be the one to make the move. For me that letter became the pointer in my memory and events were recalled always as being either 'before the letter' or 'after the letter arrived'.

It was difficult to forgive Annabel for her blunder. I could scarcely believe that personal spite and vindictiveness had prompted the act. I preferred to regard it as extreme tactlessness, and yet my common sense told me that I was ignoring the truth because I could not face all the implications of it.

The cool atmosphere which prevailed between Gavin and me made confidences impossible. He never once mentioned George Fairman's name in any connection other than the estate business affairs and his own silence made any reference to him by myself impossible.

In contrast, it seemed to me, with the deterioration in my own relationship with Gavin, Annabel's improved. Frequently she would challenge him to a game of chess during the long evenings we spent together in that drawing-room at Herren Towers. As they pitted their wits against each other I could hear the soft murmur of their voices and their mingled laughter. It was as if I were the outsider and I became increasingly conscious of the invidious position I held in the household. Sometimes I would glance up from my book to find Alice's speculative gaze fixed on me with an almost questioning air. The hours between dinnertime and bedtime took on the quality of a nightmare. I began to dread the long march of the leaden minutes and the sense of brooding oppression which gathered about me as the shadows of the evening weighed heavily upon us.

It was after one of these long drawn-out sessions when I thankfully made my escape from the room, offering an excuse that my head ached abominably and I should like an early night, that Aunt Hettie beckoned to me from her barely open doorway.

Heart sinking, as few encounters with the unbalanced old lady left me untouched by the rapier edge of her tongue, I forced a smile and crossed the hall to stand beside her. A shaft of pity stirred through me as I looked down on the top of the diminutive woman's head; it was sad that the ghosts of the past held her imprisoned by the chains of memory; even sadder that those self-same ghosts should bring her only pain for that which had gone.

'Hello, Aunt Hettie,' I greeted her with assumed cheerfulness. 'Should you not be in bed? Would you like me to fetch you a hot drink?'

She shook her head, placing her finger on her lip for silence and then gripping my wrist with a thin, talon-like hand pulling me into her room.

'Louise? That's your name, isn't it?'

Thankfully I nodded; at least she was in one of her more lucid moods and recognized me.

'I saw him . . . lurking in the grounds,' she whispered.

'Who? Who did you see, dear?' I was tired but tried to conceal my impatience with her vagaries. 'I'm sure there's nobody there.'

She nodded her head firmly. 'Yes. *He*'s there. I would never make a mistake about him, Louise. I thought he'd gone but—' her voice rose shrilly and the nails of her fingers clawed painfully into my arm—'he's come back. You know what that means, don't you?' Her eyes rolled fearfully and she cast a frightened glance over her shoulder towards the large picture window which gave on to the stone terrace.

'No. What does it mean, dear?'

I tried to draw her towards the bed in the corner, hoping to persuade her to relinquish this obsessive idea she had apparently adopted. She resisted my efforts, pulling back from me as if my touch were a red-hot brand which would sear her flesh.

'Danger.'

'Nonsense! Let me fetch you a glass of hot milk and help you into bed. I'm sure whoever you think you've seen in the garden intends no danger to you.'

'No danger to me . . . of course no danger to me. But *you*, Louise. You must be very careful.'

'I'll be careful. I promise you,' I placated her.

'You think I'm just a mad old lady,' she said, sounding tired and dispirited. I tried to argue but she went on: 'Sometimes the past is happier than the present and so I like to stay there with my memories. But not when *he's* in the garden, Louise . . . not when *he's* in the garden.'

'Perhaps you saw Harkness removing some of the garden debris,' I suggested. 'He's been working out there this afternoon.'

She threw me a petulant glare and uttered an irritated ejaculation.

'Pshaw! I know Harkness when I see him, girl.'

'Then who is this person?' I demanded. 'If you're so sure it wasn't Harkness you must

70

know who it is. What is his name?'

I saw a shuttered expression enter the crafty eyes.

'It's a name we don't mention in the house,' she muttered sullenly. 'Not since—' She broke off abruptly.

'Since when?' I prompted her.

'Since poor Miranda's accident,' she said.

To my horror I saw huge tears form in the pale, watery eyes and slowly trickle down the raddled cheeks. I felt helpless to offer any comfort to her in her distress. I toyed with the idea of fetching Gavin. She seemed to respond to him more than to any other member of the household. But I had left him playing chess with Annabel and pride made me unwilling to break up the tête-à-tête which secretly filled me with a sense of anguish I would not have revealed to a soul.

And even as I stood, helplessly looking at her, I saw the expression on her face harden.

'*You* wanted Miranda dead, didn't you?' she cried out.

'I never even knew her.'

'Miranda's watching you now . . . Miranda knows you wanted to steal her husband from her . . .'

'I tell you I never met Miranda. I never *knew* Gavin before he became a widower.' My heart was beating painfully as if I had been running. I felt my knees weaken as if they would no longer bear my weight.

71

'Liar!' she shrieked at me. 'Liar! Liar! *Liar*'

Her upraised voice brought both Gavin and Annabel at a run from the drawing-room. I stood, shaken and dismayed by the swiftness of the scene which had just taken place. It was Gavin who arrived on the spot first, his glance raking my face as if he would read the explanation for the commotion written in my features. I stared helplessly back at him, shrugging to show my own lack of understanding.

'Aunt Hettie! Calm down!' He spoke authoritatively; his manner served to quieten the screaming woman.

I began to move away from them, feeling even more of an outsider as she allowed Gavin to take her arm and, protectively holding her, lead her towards the bed. But, suddenly, she paused, turning to regard me once again, her dark eyes burning in the pallor of her face.

'*He* knows, too ... He's come for you, Louise.' She laughed shrilly and repeated: 'He's waiting for *you*, Louise. Out there ... somewhere out there! With Miranda ...'

Turning, I ran from the presence of the Summers family, seeking escape in the bedroom where I held my trembling hands to my lips to stifle my own sobs. *She was mad! I was a fool if I took notice of a mad old woman!* But I could not ignore the icy chill of fear which touched the nape of my neck, the sense of being watched which had unaccountably

72

pursued me for the last few days.

It was some time before Gavin came to bed. He looked weary and lines of strain were etched about his eyes and mouth.

'I'm sorry about all that, Louise.'

'What was it about? She mentioned a—a man in the garden . . . lurking there, she said.'

He forced a smile but it was not echoed in the eyes which he turned towards me.

'Probably Harkness.'

'I suggested it was he but she denied it.'

'Oh, Louise! You aren't taking her seriously, are you?'

'She was frightened . . . really frightened.'

'And seems to have had the same effect on you.' He laughed, a tender note in his voice to which I immediately responded as he took me in his arms. 'You're not scared, are you, Louise? Surely you're not going to allow the wild ramblings of a senile old lady to upset you, are you?'

His lips came down on mine, stilling any words I might have spoken; the warmth of his embrace reassured me, driving away the disquiet which had caused such foolish panic to surge within me. Suddenly it seemed the chasm which had separated us had disappeared; we were once more together in the bond of love which had once bound us so close.

But it was from that time I felt the sense of being watched by unseen eyes. The solitary

73

walks I had formerly taken now lost their attraction for me; in the woods I too frequently found myself glancing over my shoulder, imagining the crack of twigs beneath silent footsteps which followed in the wake of mine. Even in the house I became conscious of an oppressive, brooding air which weighed heavily on me, dulling my spirit and preventing me from taking a proper interest in my new home.

I became even more aware that I was walking in Miranda's shadow. Probably many 'second' wives are prey to secret fears and misgivings, wondering if they adequately fill the role they undertook to play; maybe there are private jealousies and anxieties which they fear to acknowledge even to themselves. But I would guarantee there are few women who carried a burden of doubts as heavy as mine ... few who felt the sense of inferiority which gradually enveloped me as, looking at Miranda's photograph, I saw the full extent of her beauty and guessed the power of her hold over Gavin's heart.

Annabel adopted a friendliness towards me which contrasted markedly with her former antagonism. I tried to meet her halfway but there was always an instinct which warned me to be on my guard. Having once fallen victim to her scheming maliciousness I was unwilling to become prey to any other tricks she might choose to use against me.

Between Alice and myself there was a sense

of acceptance and a veneer of uneasy friendship. I had detected a light of sympathy once or twice in the eyes which were so like Gavin's own. Her manner had subtly altered since the night of Aunt Hettie's wild outburst; it was almost as if she believed I needed the support of another woman in the strangely ill-assorted household. She never again mentioned George Fairman to me and I felt her sudden lack of interest concerning our friendship one of the most puzzling things at that time. She had been so ready to issue warnings earlier and yet now—?

I tried to dismiss the questions from my mind, concentrating instead on adapting to the different life entailed by moving into Herren Towers. There were endless occasions when I recalled with wistful longing the days—far-off, it seemed!—when I had been busily occupied with my work in the Brownholt Museum. Life had seemed a constant rush—never a minute to call my own. Now time hung heavily on my hands and I was tempted to write to David Ross to ask him if there were any freelance tasks which I could undertake for the Museum.

But springtime seemed to make me dilatory. As the weather improved I took my book to the cove and there, the pages remaining unread, I idled the time away as I revelled in the lullaby of the ocean as it whispered against the shingle. Occasionally George Fairman would join me for a brief while but a tension

75

had entered our relationship which had not been there in the early days.

I had told him how his letter had been opened by Annabel and the brief message misconstrued. It had embarrassed me to speak of the matter but I wanted to warn him that things were not easy up at the house.

There seemed scant surprise in his reception of my unwilling admission. He made little comment and I even found myself wondering if Gavin had already spoken of the letter to him. I could not help noticing that George made no attempt to repeat his invitation to join him in any outings and, it may have been my imagination, but I sensed a formality between us which spoilt our earlier friendship for me. The easy comradeship he had given had helped to soften my introduction into Herren Towers and I should always be grateful to him for that. I regretted the loss of his friendship and the light relief our brief encounters had afforded me.

The bluebells were spreading a carpet of blue haze beneath the trees that morning I decided to walk down to the cove through the woods. I had not followed this route so frequently recently, disliking the silence which hung heavily in the dense area. I had never been entirely able to overcome the vague misgivings which had pursued me since the night of Aunt Hettie's wild outburst. I had tried to put the incident out of mind but, despite all my efforts, I was aware that the scene had left an indelible impression on me.

But that particular morning no such unpleasant memories were niggling. I was content to enjoy the tranquillity of the surroundings as I strolled along the pathway leading to the cove. My thoughts were occupied with a letter from David Ross which had arrived by the morning delivery. He discussed a new project put forward by the Guardians of the Brownholt Trust; briefly the idea was that a group of Egyptologists should travel to Luxor for two months under the auspices of the Museum in order to enquire into the possibility of setting up an exchange working party. David wanted to put my name forward as a member of the prospective team but, before doing so, he had decided to seek my reaction to the suggestion.

How tempting I should have found this invitation so short a time ago! I thought. And had it come much earlier in the year might it not even have affected my decision to marry Gavin? The question surprised me, unexpectedly halting my progress along the tree-fringed path.

I wondered how Gavin would take it if I were to tell him that I was considering going— and suddenly it occurred to me that I was actually giving serious thought to David's letter.

Perhaps a brief absence from Gavin might

help to improve the atmosphere which had built up between us; distance would perhaps offer to both of us the opportunity to put our relationship into its correct perspective. Somehow the love which had once bound us together had been pushed into the background by the affairs of Herren Towers and the estate. Miranda felt too near us and I was unpleasantly aware of a feeling that I had stolen Gavin from her. It was absurd, I knew. But I could not escape it.

Oh, but I couldn't—I couldn't possibly consider leaving Gavin for two whole months! The idea of being away from him for that length of time appalled me—filled me with a sense of loneliness.

Once more I started to make my way along the sun-dappled path, putting David's letter out of mind as I regarded with pleasure the many signs of approaching summer. The fresh green leaves on the trees, the smell of the turf beneath my feet and, in the distance, the constant murmuring of the sea as it broke on the sandy cove at the foot of the cliffs.

Then, even as I listened to that distant sound of ocean meeting shore, I heard the voices upraised in argument.

I paused, frozen to the spot, recognizing Gavin's low tones mingling with those of a stranger.

'I told you never to come here again,' I heard Gavin say. 'Get off my property and keep away from any member of my family.'

'Especially that beautiful new wife of yours, I suppose!' came the jeering reply.

'Leave Louise out of this.' Gavin's voice was harsh, hatred in its depths.

'Of course, old man. Just as you say,' the smooth tones of the stranger returned. 'We wouldn't want her to learn too much about Miranda's accident, would we? She might get a little anxious about her own pretty neck if you should chance to tire of her in a few months' time.'

CHAPTER EIGHT

'Why, you—' There was the sound of a scuffle, rustlings amongst the bushes, heavy breathing.

I wanted to run to the clearing where the unseen men were engaged in their brief skirmish but those last words had paralysed my limbs. I was atrophied to the spot as the full horror of the stranger's mocking sentence penetrated. What did he mean by his cryptic statement? I could feel my own breath coming more quickly as my heart pounded in an excess of fear.

'Now, Gavin, don't let's resort to schoolboy violence. I've told you what I want.' The last words were rapped out with the velocity of a burst of machine-gun fire.

'And I've told you I don't intend to pay you blackmail money.'

'That's a naughty little word, old man. Well—' the voice regained its former suave tone—'you mustn't blame me if Louise gets to hear a few home truths about you.'

'And *you* mustn't blame me if I break your bloody neck for you if I ever catch you anywhere near my wife!'

'Threats ... threats ... threats! You're rather given to issuing them, aren't you? That's why Miranda was afraid of you, wasn't it?'

'That's a damned lie, Travers, and you know it. She never feared me.'

'That's not what she led me to believe.'

I moved a step or two forwards on the path, careful now to remain concealed by the trees and heavy underbrush, trying not to allow my footsteps to give away my presence; I felt no compunction in eavesdropping on this quarrel not intended for my ears.

Through a gap in the branches I could see the two men. Gavin's back was towards me, his head thrust forward belligerently. The other man was facing him, a wary expression in his eyes despite the mocking smile he wore on his thin lips. Lantern-jawed with hollow cheeks, there was an air of slyness about him which made me instinctively distrust him. I noticed that he was careful to maintain his distance as if fearing an unexpected attack upon his person.

'Get off my property before I throw you off!' Gavin's voice held a steel-like quality. 'I'll give you just five minutes to get out of my sight.'

'Aren't you interested in hearing what Miranda told me, Gavin?'

'I am not.'

'Then you will let me have the money, won't you? I'll make everything public unless you—'

Gavin made a move towards him. The stranger took a hurried step back and started to make his way from the clearing towards the path where I was standing. I hurried back in the direction from which I'd come when I chanced upon this unexpected scene. I heard no more of their talk and, with a sigh of relief, I saw that the man called Travers was going in the direction away from the house. There was no sign of Gavin.

I gave the stranger a minute or two to get clear and then I started to retrace my steps. At the clearing, I paused. Gavin was sitting on the stump of a sawn-off tree, his head cushioned in his hands, an air of dejection about him. I stood for a moment watching him, my heart stirring with pity.

It seemed that the confrontation with Mr. Travers had not left him completely untouched. I supposed that it must be the echoes from the past which had evoked the melancholy which clearly weighed him down. I felt a stab of jealousy once more, thinking of the unknown Miranda whose place in his life I had taken.

I moved, and a twig on the path snapped beneath my foot. Gavin raised his head, swiftly masking his feelings as he looked up, meeting my eyes. He smiled, getting to his feet as I approached; had I not witnessed for myself that recent scene, his attitude would not have given me occasion to believe there was anything amiss.

'Louise! I thought you would already be sitting in your favourite spot in the cove by now. You're late this morning.'

'I—I stopped to talk to Harkness about the azaleas,' I said, then, taking a deep breath, I went on: 'Who was that man, Gavin?'

'Man? What man?' His expression was innocent, bland.

'I—I thought you were talking to somebody in the clearing. I heard voices in the distance and then—then I saw a man on the path in front of me.'

'Oh, yes ... *that* man.' He laughed easily. 'Just a tourist, darling. The season's beginning now. He'd taken the wrong path and wandered on to private property without realizing it. He wanted to get back to the road so I gave him directions.'

I turned away, suddenly feeling sick. Gavin had deliberately lied to me.

CHAPTER NINE

'Dear David,

'Thanks for your letter—' I wrote—*'and the invitation to join the team travelling out to Egypt. I'll be delighted to go with them.'*

A few more lines and the letter was completed. I sealed the envelope with a sense of having come to a momentous decision.

I had still made no reference to Gavin about the proposed tour and, in view of his own secrecy, I felt no sense of guilt regarding my silence. All day long the memory of that small scene on which I'd accidentally stumbled had remained in the background of my thoughts.

The fact that he should have chosen to lie to me had shocked me to the core. It added an importance to the overheard remarks with all their veiled innuendo which had not been there previously. Again and again I relived the sick horror which had filled me at his words . . . the bland way in which he had forestalled any further questioning by a smooth change of conversation.

Those few minutes had served to turn Gavin into a stranger. I felt a need to get away from him in order to consider the situation between us; pretend to others as I might, I could no longer deceive myself about the sour note which had entered our marriage. Since the night of our arrival in Herren Towers circumstances had been steadily worsening. I had been conscious of an enmity and hostility surrounding me which had finally infiltrated the love I felt for Gavin.

I did not fool myself for one moment that the love had been destroyed. But the protective barrier it had afforded me against the hurt from other members of the Summers family had weakened against the constant pressures. I was aware of a need to escape before my love was diminished by the influence of life here at Herren Towers.

It seemed a fortuitous coincidence that David's letter offered me the chance to get away for a brief period, even furnishing me with a reason which I believed Gavin would understand.

I did not think he would try to stop me going. He did not believe that a woman automatically relinquished her individuality from the time a wedding band was placed on her left hand and he knew that my career had been important to me.

As I slipped the envelope into my handbag, making a mental note to post it next time I walked into the village, I even felt a sense of anticipation at the prospect of the Egyptian trip.

I would tell Gavin what I had done when a suitable opportunity presented itself. There seemed few enough chances to talk with each other these days but there was no immediate rush, after all. I should not be going for a few weeks anyway. I would wait for David Ross's confirmation that the Board of Guardians had definitely included my name as a member of the team before telling Gavin my intention.

Meanwhile the vexing question of the mysterious stranger's presence in the wood continued to nag at me with troublesome persistence despite my attempts to put it out of mind. Clearly it would be useless to question Gavin any further about the matter and I felt unwilling to broach the subject either to Annabel or Alice.

Perhaps it was this reluctance which made me more willing to mention the stranger's presence to George Fairman when I chanced to meet him down in the cove two days after the incident.

Strolling along the shore I tried to frame the question in words which would not sound as if I were trying to snoop into family matters which were none of my concern. But finally, throwing discretion to the winds, I asked my question point blank.

'George, have you ever heard of a man called Travers?'

I thought he uttered a muffled oath, then: 'What do you know about Ed Travers, Louise?'

'Nothing. That's why I'm asking you about him.'

'Where have you heard of him?'

There was a steel-hardness to his features

which I'd never seen before on the genial bailiff's face; his lips were compressed firmly, his eyes sharp, scrutinizing, as he waited for my reply.

'He—he was in the woods the other day,' I answered, hesitantly.

'*Here?*' He appeared astounded, actually pausing a moment in mid-step before resuming his easy pace beside me.

'Yes.'

'Did he make himself known to you?'

'No.'

'Then how do you know it was Ed?'

'I overheard Gavin address him as Travers.'

'*Gavin*! He spoke to him?'

'There—there was a quarrel. I chanced to come on them in the middle of a most terrible argument. I thought they'd come to blows.'

'It wouldn't be the first time,' he said drily.

'Who is he?'

'Didn't Gavin tell you when you asked him?' he countered.

'If you must know he—he lied to me. He told me that the man he'd been talking to was a stranger who'd walked into the Herren property by accident. But, George, I'd heard Gavin call him Travers and tell him never to come here again. There was talk of—blackmail . . .'

This time I actually heard the expletive George muttered beneath his breath.

'He spoke about Miranda's accident,' I went on, 'as if Gavin had something to hide.'

'That swine would!' he said. 'Forget it, Louise. It's nothing for you to worry about.'

'Then why did Gavin consider it necessary to lie to me, George?'

He looked uncomfortable. 'That's hardly a fair question to put to me. You'll have to tax him with it.'

'But I've already told you. He denied that he knew the man.'

'You'll have to tell him you overheard the conversation then, won't you?'

'He'll believe I was ... spying on him,' I said, unwillingly.

George shrugged. 'Get it out in the open, Louise. Ed Travers is trouble for Gavin. He's trying to shield you ... protect you ...'

'But there's no necessity for protection,' I protested angrily.

'Tell Gavin that, not me. If you must know, Ed is a distant relative of Miranda's. He was always hanging around her. There was trouble even when she was alive. Gavin couldn't stand the sight of him.'

I felt my heart lower even further. Jealous? Had Gavin been jealous of Ed Travers? It sounded suspiciously like it. The thought hurt, cutting through to some inner guard with which I tried to protect myself from these spectres of the past.

'Was he—jealous?' I asked, reluctantly. 'Was

87

Gavin jealous?'

'How the hell do I know?' He stopped abruptly in his tracks, turning to face me. 'You'll have to ask him about that, too.'

His expression sombre, he reached out a hand and drew me nearer. I felt comforted by the warmth and bulk of the man, sensing a strength in him which my own lack of it recognized in that split second. He stared down into my face for a moment and, when he spoke, his voice was harsh, vehement.

'God! He's a damned fool. If you were *my* woman, Louise, I'd never risk losing you.'

Before I knew what he was about, George's arms had circled round me, his lips closed on mine, the pressure bruising as he kissed me with an almost desperate intensity. Weak as I was at that time, cut off from Gavin as I felt, there was comfort in that embrace and I felt my physical senses answer to the ardour of George's unexpected kiss. Sensing my response George lifted his mouth from mine to murmur: 'Louise! Louise! I never dreamed—I didn't intend—' But the sentence unfinished, his lips met mine again and once more we were transported on the crest of that rising wave of passion which our closeness aroused.

The embers of our mutual attraction for each other flamed into a furnace for those few seconds before common sense—and the memory of Gavin—returned to me.

I pulled away from George. The passion he

had aroused within me now as swiftly ebbing as humiliation suffused me. What of my love for Gavin? Could it be so swiftly forgotten in the warmth of someone else's kisses?

Even as I took a step backwards, I saw that George, too, was equally shamefaced. He tried to stammer an apology but I cut across it with swift words of dismissal, almost running away from him in my urgent need to remove myself from his presence there in the cove. I was afraid that one touch of his hand might still send my senses reeling; weak and lonely it would be so easy to seek solace with George's comforting personality. But for any temporary consolation he might offer me, the price would be too high to pay. Gavin might no longer want my love, but, nevertheless, it was a gift I should bring him, unsullied and unfaltering, until eternity itself.

*   *   *

Back at Herren Towers I felt confused. That brief moment in the cove with George had served to emphasize the uncertainty of my situation and emotions. I felt as if I skirted invisible quicksands, not knowing if any step I took would cause me to sink into depths from which I could not escape. I needed to be alone to sort out my own feelings and place a tighter control on myself. I planned to go to my room, knowing that Gavin was out and there at least I should have a little solitude while I tried to gather myself together.

Crossing the main hall towards the staircase I chanced to glance at the large hall table as I passed by. The letter addressed to *'Mrs. Louise Summers'* had been placed in a prominent position—probably by Annabel who usually made an ostentatious show of handing me my mail personally since the earlier disagreement we'd had over George's note.

I did not recognize the bold handwriting and picked the envelope up with a flickering curiosity.

Opening it in the bedroom, I scanned the words swiftly until I came to the signature. Then I took in a deep breath and started to read the letter again, more slowly this time.

'Dear Louise—' it began—

'I hope you will forgive a stranger addressing you with such familiarity. But as we are almost related to each other by your marriage to Gavin it would seem undue formality to call you anything other.

'My dear, my presence has never been made welcome at Herren Towers so I am unable to call and pay my respects on you. I am, however, staying for a few weeks at Hope Cottage—only a mile or so away—and I should be so glad if you would come and share a pot of tea with me tomorrow afternoon. I have matters to discuss with you which cannot be written about. I assure

you that what I have to say is important and may affect your entire future. I beg your indulgence and also your discretion. It would be inadvisable for you to mention this invitation to any of the Summers family who would most assuredly forbid you to visit!

'Margaret Travers.'

Travers? Margaret *Travers* . . .? It could be no coincidence. Was she Ed Travers's wife? She spoke of being unwelcome at Herren Towers so it was possible that Gavin's hostility to Ed extended itself also to this mysterious stranger who wrote to me as if we shared a common bond.

Perhaps it was that remark about the Summers family 'forbidding' me to visit my unknown correspondent which filled me with defiance! I do not know. I was only certain that, come hell or high water, I should visit Hope Cottage on the morrow and, obeying the urge for discretion, I was determined to make no mention of the surprising letter which had apparently been delivered by hand.

Half expecting veiled curiosity about it over dinner with the family that evening, I was surprised that no mention was made of that important-looking envelope. The question was cleared for me later by Mrs. Harkness when we were alone. She asked me if I'd found the letter on the hall table. She explained that it had been delivered by a youth from the village and, as she'd guessed I would shortly be back, she had left it where I should be most likely to find it on my return.

The following afternoon I left the house without encountering any of the family. Walking down the drive, the sharp breeze blowing my hair into disarray, I was conscious of a sense of relief that I had been faced with no necessity to prevaricate about my destination.

I was filled with curiosity about Margaret Travers and eager to make her acquaintance. I had a vague idea where Hope Cottage was situated and a few minutes' brisk walk brought me within sight of the small detached stone cottage set in a typical country garden.

There was nothing particularly attractive about the place and, as I walked up the narrow path to the front door, I had the unpleasant sensation of being watched by unseen eyes. Instinctively I looked towards the window nearest the door and was just in time to see an abrupt movement as if somebody had jumped back from view the second before my glance had travelled in that direction. I felt a swift compunction that I had impulsively come to the cottage at the whim of a stranger, disliking the sense of being spied upon. Perhaps I should have been better advised to have told Gavin of Margaret Travers' invitation after all! But I was here now and, as I raised my hand to the tiny knocker set high on the solid oak door,

I drew in a deep breath or two, hoping to calm the sudden panic which had threatened me.

CHAPTER TEN

Almost as soon as my hand had left the knocker, the door was opened. The petite figure of the elderly woman who stood on the threshold was sufficient to disperse all those weird apprehension. I felt the tension fade as I relaxed in the warmth of her friendly welcome.

'You must be Louise! Oh, my dear! I'm so pleased to meet you. Do please come in! I hope you had no difficulty in finding your way here. A charming cottage but, I must admit, it looks very like every other cottage in this locality.' Even as she spoke, her words coming quickly, eagerly, she was drawing me into the narrow hallway, her plump hands grasping mine warmly. 'Come into the sitting-room. But let me take your coat first, child. There! Hang it over that hook. How pretty you are, Louise! I can see why Gavin lost his heart to you.'

I took off my jacket and placed it on the coat-stand. I noticed there was a man's jacket already hanging there. Ed Travers's? Probably.

Following my loquacious hostess into the sitting-room—on the opposite side of the hall to the room where I had glimpsed that furtive movement at the window—I realized I had

93

hardly been given the opportunity to do more than smile and nod occasionally. She kept up a steady flow of inconsequential chatter—about the weather . . . the estate . . . the crops . . . the number of tourists descending in their droves on the nearby town.

As she talked she patted the cushions of a capacious armchair, settling me into it with a motherly concern for my comfort. I was beginning to feel a trifle bewildered by her ministrations, my head reeling with the effort of following her swift changes of subject.

It was not until my hostess was pouring out our tea that she offered me the first real opportunity to join in the conversation.

'I expect you were surprised to receive a letter from *me*, weren't you, Louise?'

She cast me a sidelong smile as she handed me the cup and saucer. I placed it on the small table she had set beside me, not wanting her to notice the giveaway tremor of my hand as I wondered about the reason for this meeting.

'Yes, I was rather,' I answered, non-committally. A tiny warning note told me to say as little as possible.

'I suppose my name must be avoided at Herren Towers, of course.'

She waited a moment, giving me an opportunity to enlarge on the subject. I smiled politely, disparagingly, saying nothing.

With a vaguely disappointed air, she went on: 'Ever since the accident we've been

94

unwelcome at the house.'

'We?' I questioned.

'My son and I,' she enlarged. 'I suppose Ed was too outspoken for Gavin's liking, that was the trouble. He's too high and mighty for his own good,' she added spitefully.

'Your son?' I wilfully misunderstood her, feeling a certain disloyalty in listening to this woman's opinion of my husband.

I was aware that, in spite of her friendliness and gushing manner, I did not like Margaret Travers any more than did Gavin like her unpleasant son.

'Gavin, of course.' She gave me an angry glance, but quickly disguised it.

'Why should Gavin resent anybody being outspoken?' I asked. 'I've always found that he respects another person's viewpoint and admires them for expressing it without fear or favour.'

'Provided that viewpoint doesn't affect him personally, my dear.'

Leaning forward, she offered me a buttered scene with a blob of strawberry jam perched rakishly on it; she carefully prodded the jam into a more secure position with a small knife like an artist with a palette knife. I refused the scone automatically, registering the fact that she took it herself, crumbling it into pieces on her plate as if it gave her fidgety fingers something to do.

'I don't agree with you. Gavin is one of the

fairest men I've ever met,' I maintained obstinately.

'That isn't the opinion Miranda held.' Margaret Travers's expression was lugubrious, her tone solemn as a church bell. 'But then— perhaps you didn't know Miranda well, did you?'

'No. I never knew her. I didn't meet Gavin until last autumn.'

'Oh? You surprise me . . . I thought that you were probably an—old friend of his.'

'I can't think what can have given you that impression.'

But couldn't I just . . .! The spiteful old harridan was surely suggesting that I had been Gavin's mistress during Miranda's lifetime. I clung tightly to my temper, determined not to leave Hope Cottage until I understood the reason for the invitation. I was sure Margaret Travers had not invited me simply to look me over.

'Ah! What a pity you never met her.' She sighed gustily. 'She was beautiful . . . truly beautiful.'

'So I believe. I've seen her photograph, of course. And Annabel bears such a remarkable resemblance to her that—'

'Annabel . . . *That* one.' The sudden animosity in her voice surprised me. 'Like chalk and cheese in nature. Miranda was gentle and kind. That other one is totally ignorant of the meaning of the words.'

96

'You sound as if you were very fond of Miranda,' I ventured.

'Fond of her? Of course I was fond of her. My only brother's daughter . . . Should I not be fond of her?'

'Your brother's daughter?' I tried to hide my surprise but could not entirely conceal it.

'Of course. Didn't you know?' The surprise was now apparent in Margaret Travers' tone, too.

'I wasn't certain exactly what the relationship was,' I prevaricated. 'Then Annabel, too, is related to you?'

'Yes, but she's one of *them* now. She sides with them . . . has no room for us.'

'Them? You mean the Summers family?'

She nodded. 'When Miranda was killed so tragically it was as if I lost both girls at the same time. But still—I have to learn to live with the sorrow. Family differences can take much time to heal.'

'But why should Annabel have turned away from her own relatives to ally herself with those linked to her only by her cousin's marriage? Surely the bond cannot be particularly strong in those circumstances.'

'You may well ask, dear Louise. You may well ask.' She raised a beseeching glance heavenwards as if expecting intervention from that source. 'It is sad, isn't it? But the young are so impetuous . . . so headstrong . . . so set in their views.'

'I wouldn't describe Annabel as an impulsive person,' I argued. 'She strikes me as a person whose moves are carefully premeditated ... whose plans are made only after thought and consideration.'

'Shrewd of you, my dear. In this instance, the plan was to marry Gavin. Your unexpected arrival on the scene rather threw a spanner into the works.'

'I still don't understand why her personal wishes should affect her relationship with you,' I objected.

She gave me a surprised, slightly irritated, glance. 'But after the circumstances of dear Miranda's fatal accident she could hardly side with us and then marry him, could she? Oh, I know that the Coroner's Court exonerated him from all blame but—Well ...' her voice trailed off—'there's no smoke without fire, is there?'

The clichés were coming thick and fast but I was too bemused to do more than grasp at the main drift of her words. Coroner's Court ...? Blame ...? Exonerated him ...? The echo of her words rang again and again in my ears. I felt a trifle light-headed but fought to keep my dumbfounded emotions hidden from the pale eyes which continued to watch me shrewdly.

'I don't understand ... I ...' My words faltered. I realized I was perhaps giving away more than I intended concerning my ignorance about the particular circumstances of Miranda's death.

'Do you mean to tell me you didn't know that Gavin was involved? He must have taken the life-jackets from the boat. Talk had it that they'd been quarrelling frequently during the preceding weeks. They say that had there been a life-jacket aboard, she might have been saved when the boat capsized. He denied it all at the inquest but?' She shrugged before continuing: 'My Ed had been with Miranda only the previous day . . . They'd gone for a short trip and she made him wear a life-jacket then because he can't swim. Gavin must have removed the life-jackets after he'd seen them return to shore together.'

I made no reply; my thoughts were a circling vortex without beginning or end. I was more aware of feeling than logic or reason in those unforgettable moments of revelation.

'Poor Louise! He should have told you the truth. If it isn't just like Gavin . . . Always determined to gain his own way without thought for anyone else.' Her voice was tinged with sympathy but it was belied by the hint of mockery I saw in her eyes. After an almost imperceptible pause, she went on: 'Well, it would seem my intention in inviting you here is entirely unnecessary, my dear.'

'Exactly *why* did you ask me to come?' I demanded.

'I wanted to try to set your mind at ease regarding Gavin.'

'It was never anything other than at ease,' I

said coolly.

'They do say that where ignorance is bliss it's folly to be wise. I had assumed that he would have had the decency to tell you the truth regarding his share of the blame over his first wife's accident. I wanted to tell you that we—her family—in no way hold him responsible or bear him any grudge.'

Not much! I thought cynically, remembering Ed's threats in the wood—threats which had not been intended for other ears than Gavin's.

Aloud I said: 'I'm sure he'll be relieved to know that.' I took a sip or two of tea, nearly cold now. It tasted bitter, unpleasant, and I replaced the cup and saucer on the table.

She seemed not to notice the sarcasm of my tones as she beamed brightly at me. 'Good. Now we understand each other better, don't we?'

'I think we understand each other very well,' I said sharply. 'And now, Mrs. Travers, if you'll excuse me, I think I had better get back to the house.' I started to rise to my feet as she uttered a tiny shriek of dismay.

'Oh, Louise!' Her expression was reproachful. 'You can't possibly leave here without meeting my son, Ed. You'd both have so much in common, I'm sure.'

'*So much in common*!' The words echoed in my mind as sudden revulsion for this woman . . . this cottage . . . even my own foolishness in coming here . . . filled me.

'I have to go now,' I said abruptly, without apology.

'Then you'll come again, won't you? Perhaps next week . . .? I'll get Ed to pick you up at the gates of Herren Towers—' her smile was sly— 'or perhaps somewhere a little more discreet if you're anxious to avoid Gavin finding out we're such good friends now.'

I stared at her without really seeing her; her absurd words circled repetitiously as I turned and made my way towards the door.

Walking down the path to the gate, I felt again the sensation of unseen eyes following my progress from behind those curtained windows. I turned sharply, looking over my shoulder. Margaret Travers stood framed in the doorway, smiling in a sugary fashion at my departing back. She gave a tiny wave of her pudgy, beringed hand, but I feigned not to notice it and made my way out of the garden into the lane beyond. Suddenly the air felt cleaner, purer. I breathed deeply, my thoughts gripping me in a nightmare hold.

Gavin . . .? Was it true that he had been inadvertently responsible for Miranda's accident? Did this explain his moods of reserve? Did this account for the distance he seemed to have placed between us?

And had it been an innocent oversight . . . a human error which could be made by anybody? Margaret Travers had insinuated that it was perhaps more than accidental. But it was ridiculous. A ludicrous suggestion which could have no grain of truth in it . . . could it . . .?

The poison was festering.

CHAPTER ELEVEN

Only when I was again back in Herren Towers did I remember the letter to David Ross which I had slipped into my handbag intending to pop it in the mail box near Hope Cottage. Annoyed at my own absent-mindedness I took the sealed envelope from the compartment in my bag and placed it on the dressing-table. I should see it there when I went out next and resolved to hold it in my hand all the way to the pillarbox! That way I should be sure that I shouldn't again forget to post it.

It still wanted an hour or so until I could begin to change for dinner with the family. How slowly these leisurely days passed! I sighed. The memory of the afternoon tea party with Margaret Travers still lingered uncomfortably. I felt ruffled and the idea of a walk in the grounds appealed strongly. Perhaps I might find the tranquillity of the terraced gardens soothing to my unquiet spirit.

The spring day was pleasantly warm, and stopping only long enough to collect a woolly, I hurried back down the stairs and out of the front door. On the stone terrace I hesitated, wondering which direction to take.

The woods were repugnant to me now. Since that overheard conversation between Gavin and Ed Travers I imagined I felt a sense of threat and impending doom in the heavy shadows cast there by the giant trees. I wondered, too, if I should run into George Fairman if I made my way down to the cove. I was in no mood for company, preferring to reflect on the unexpected events of the afternoon at Hope Cottage.

So it was that my footsteps took me through the terraced rose arbour, neatly trimmed and pruned rose bushes lining the way in elegant profusion; past the tennis courts and down to the small lake, glistening like a silver mirror in the late afternoon sunlight. There, slipping my woolly cardigan over my shoulders to counteract the rising breeze, I sat on the wooden bench which gave a view of the green undulating hills which cocooned Herren Towers within a valley. I felt the sense of timelessness cast by the scenery gradually drive away the anger and bitterness which had been building up inside me.

But human emotions can never long be absent and, as the rancour faded, so my inner sense of confusion increased. The turmoil of my mixed emotions welled up inside me and I became even more deeply conscious of the great gulf which now separated Gavin and me.

Margaret Travers had spoken of frequent quarrels between Miranda and Gavin. It was the first I had heard of them; indeed, all references to their marriage had given the impression of an idyllic partnership and eternal honeymoon. I felt the snaking jealousy stir in me once again and, unwilling to recognize the emotion for what it was, I forced my errant thoughts back to the tragic accident which had brought their marriage to its premature end. I was the trespasser, intruding into Gavin's grief and loneliness. Probably it had been only a physical attraction which had ever drawn him to me when we had first met in the Brownholt Museum. Now—in the place where memories of his former happiness surrounded him—he realized that he had made a mistake in marrying me.

I was filled with a sense of desolation and loss. It was as if Gavin had told me all his feelings, I understood them so clearly. No wonder we had felt estranged from each other!

Miranda! Everywhere I looked I seemed to see her ghost approaching me. It was as if she were constantly present, trying to drive her presence like a wedge between us. I knew that it would be foolish for me to hope that Gavin would ever feel such a depth of love for me. His loyalty would prevent him from causing me hurt by telling me the truth about his feelings but did I want to continue a marriage farce with a man who no longer had need of me?

Then I saw Miranda herself walking across the garden towards me . . . My blood ran cold, my hands tensed . . . And then common sense returned as I realized it must be Annabel who, seeing me alone here, had decided to join me.

'Hello, Louise! Aren't you cold? There's a breeze sprung up now and you're not wearing a coat.'

Her solicitude sat oddly with the customary animosity I had come to expect but her face gave no indication of her thoughts. She wore a short camel-hair coat over a plaid skirt; her dark hair was caught back in a neat chignon, emphasizing the large, luminous eyes, deeply shadowed, whether by design or chance I could not tell.

'I'm quite cosy, thanks. But—' glancing at my watch I saw that time had flown while I had been sitting here—'it's time I went back to the house anyway. I have to shower and change.'

I got up, suddenly reluctant to leave this peaceful spot and return to the house where the complex emotions of the Summers family cast a brooding atmosphere over everything.

'I was on my way back so let's go together.' Annabel fell into step beside me. 'I've just been for a stroll down to the village and I thought I'd come home by way of the field path. It's pleasant enough in summer but the ground's so wet I began to wish I was wearing Wellies.'

I looked down at Annabel's dainty feet and

saw they were shod in fashionable suède court shoes which by no stretch of the imagination could be regarded as suitable for a country stroll. Heavy mud encased them. I privately doubted whether any amount of brushing would ever restore them to their former condition.

'I don't think it's done your shoes much good.'

She glanced down and smiled ruefully. 'No, you're right. Never mind! My afternoon jaunt was worth a pair of shoes.'

There was a self-satisfied air about her which surprised me. Her mood earlier in the day had been considerably less cheerful. I wondered what had happened to imbue her with such good humour that she was even willing to display an unaccustomed friendliness towards me.

'Oh? What made it so successful?'

Her eyes narrowed sharply. 'Why should anything have happened to make it successful?' she demanded.

Surprised at her question, I hesitated for a moment. 'I just thought—the way you spoke— it sounded as if something special had happened.'

'I just chanced to see—' she paused—'an old friend.'

I had a sudden suspicion that she knew the Travers were in residence at Hope Cottage. Perhaps she even knew that I had visited there earlier in the afternoon?

I wondered if she'd followed me but dismissed the thought as unworthy.

'How nice for you!' I spoke automatically, wondering why she made such a point of telling me about it.

'Nice for *me* perhaps—' she paused, smiling secretively—'but I'm not so sure Gavin will be pleased to hear who is back in the village.'

I knew she was referring to Margaret and Ed Travers now but I didn't believe she was aware of my own presence in Hope Cottage earlier in the afternoon.

'Why? Who is this old friend of yours?' I probed.

'He's—' She broke off abruptly, then: 'Oh, I'm sorry, Louise!' she said. 'How boring for you! All this discussion about somebody you've never met!'

'Naturally I'm curious about the person now you mention Gavin's displeasure at his re-appearance.'

'Oh, Ed and Gavin have always been at daggers drawn—ever since Gavin caught Ed kissing Miranda in the boat-house. There was a dreadful scene there. George Fairman had to intervene. If he hadn't I believe Gavin would have murdered Ed in his jealousy.' She drew in her breath swiftly, clapping her hand to her mouth. 'Oh dear! My tongue runs away with me sometimes. You won't ever let on to Gavin that I've told you about the incident, will you?'

I shook my head, too flabbergasted to do more. The revelation that Miranda and her cousin were enjoying a slightly less than innocent relationship certainly went quite a way to explain the enmity which existed between the two men.

I decided it was time to reveal my own knowledge about the Travers' ménage; meagre though it was it seemed unwise to maintain secrecy about it.

'Do you mean Ed Travers?'

She turned to me in surprise. 'You know him?'

'No, but I had an invitation from Margaret Travers to have tea at Hope Cottage this afternoon. I didn't meet her son though.'

'You *went*?' She appeared astounded.

'Why should I not have done?'

'Did Gavin know?'

'No.'

'I shouldn't tell him, if I were you.'

'But *why*?'

'I've already told you the two men loathe each other and Margaret Travers has never done much to repair the breach. Let's just call it a family feud and leave it at that, shall we, Louise? But it would be wiser not to let him know you've met the notorious Travers unless you want to let all hell loose on your head.'

'Thanks for the tip,' I said non-committally, intending to tell Gavin at the first opportunity that I had been to Hope Cottage and what had

108

transpired. I was not over enthusiastic about keeping secrets which might rebound on me.

We were within sight of the house now and a sudden silence fell between us; it was as if the sight of the grey, gaunt house reminded us both of the chain of circumstances which had led to my own arrival in it. I was once again made instantly aware of the presence of Miranda; it was as if her physical shape was actually with us as we neared Herren Towers and my spirit felt vaguely chilled, a sense of depression weighed heavily on my shoulders.

Nevertheless, I was relieved that this enforced period of intimacy with Annabel was coming to an end. I was unaccustomed to sharing confidences with her as if we were bosom pals and could not escape the warning presentiment that she knew far more than she had told me about the Travers and the quarrel with Gavin.

Impulsively, I said: 'She was telling me that Gavin had been inadvertently to blame for Miranda's death as he had removed the life-jackets from the boat. At least, to be accurate, she was saying he shouldn't consider himself to blame and she held no personal animosity for his part in the accident. But the Coroner's Court had—'

Suddenly Annabel turned towards me, her attitude that of a virago, her face contorted with rage. 'Shut up!' she ordered, between gritted teeth. 'Shut up! You don't know anything about it! You're interfering in matters which are none of your concern. You forced your way into the house by catching Gavin on the rebound and now—' Her words ended in a choked sob as she spun on her heels and, wheeling around, retraced her steps down the drive.

Bewildered, I stopped to stare after her retreating back. I had not known what to expect after my disclosure but I had decidedly not anticipated Annabel's wild outburst. I hesitated a moment, wondering if I should go after her, then, shrugging slightly as I realized I might only make matters worse, I turned and made my way into the house.

*   *   *

Perturbed by the unexpected climax to the strange afternoon, I decided to go straight upstairs to our room to change for the evening meal. I crossed the hall quietly, hoping that Aunt Hettie would not be listening behind her door, waiting to trap the unwary like a spider in its web waiting for the innocent fly.

I felt compassion for the frail, old woman with her bemused mind, but I could not hide the fact that any session with her left me with the impression that I was an interloper in Herren Towers. She never concealed the resentment she held for me because I had usurped Miranda's position in the house. She invariably spoke of Gavin's first wife as if she were still alive and would soon return to claim her rightful position at Gavin's side. It was uncanny and intensified my own feelings of rejection by the Summers family.

As I climbed the stairs I heard Alice talking with Philip in the small sitting-room. I could not make out the words but, if I were to judge by the low murmur of their voices, it sounded as if they were in deep discussion.

Philip had always maintained a friendly air and he was the one person in this strangely assorted household with whom I felt completely at ease. I could not understand why Gavin seemed to hold his younger brother in such disapproval. There seemed always an aura of cool disapprobation in his manner whenever Philip's name entered the conversation; there was a reserve in their contacts with each other which occasionally made itself felt like a tangible blanket weighing heavily on the atmosphere.

But my mind was not concerned with these minor trivialities when I opened the door of the room I shared with Gavin, and went inside.

Pausing a moment there I had a swift instinct that somebody else had recently left the room; it was as if an impression had been left on the air itself like an invisible fingerprint on the ether.

I could not explain the reason for the conviction. I was only certain that a short while previously a stranger had stood in this very room—perhaps on the self-same spot on which I now stood myself. Gradually the awareness faded as I moved further into the room.

It was a full minute before I noticed that the letter I had written to David Ross and forgotten to post was now missing from the dressing-table where I had placed it before going out in the gardens. Almost at the same moment, I saw the mud traces on the light carpet. Mud which had fallen from some intruder's shoes when he—or she—had crossed the room to look more closely at the letter I'd put there.

And whose footwear had been sufficiently dirty to leave those marks behind? I remembered the state of Annabel's dainty shoes and was in no doubt as to the identity of the person who had entered this room and stolen my letter.

CHAPTER TWELVE

In my anger I was determined to confront Annabel with the theft of the letter to David Ross.

I waited until I guessed she would be back in her room changing and, as I hurried along the corridor, I could feel my rage rising. Without pausing for thought I tapped loudly on her door, scarcely waiting for her to call 'Come in'.

I opened the door and marched inside. She was sitting at her dressing-table, coiling her long hair into a chignon; surprised at my abrupt entry she lost her grasp on it and the silky smooth locks fell back on to her shoulders. I heard her mutter a tiny imprecation beneath her breath as she looked to see who had entered

'Where is my letter, Annabel?' I demanded, without any preliminaries. 'I want it back, please.'

She pretended to look puzzled, gazing at me with an assumed air of bewilderment as she swivelled around to face me.

'Letter? I don't know what you're talking about, Louise. What letter do you mean?'

'You know very well. The one you stole from my dressing-table before you found me in the garden this afternoon.'

Her eyes hardened momentarily. 'Are you accusing me of *stealing* something from your room?' she asked, her tones quietly controlled although I could see that anger now raged beneath the calm exterior she had turned towards me.

'Don't let's play games, Annabel,' I snapped. 'Please give me back the letter you took from my dressing-table.'

'I've taken no letter of yours, sweetie,' she said, her manner tinged with sympathy. 'Poor Louise! You have been looking a trifle overwrought recently. I expect you absent-mindedly put it down somewhere and now you—'

'I put it on the dressing-table,' I said obstinately. 'Don't treat me as if I'm as mad as Aunt Hettie.'

'Naughty, naughty Louise!' she returned, playfully. 'We all know about Aunt Hettie but we don't speak of her affliction quite so cruelly as that, dear.'

Languorously she started to brush her hair, each movement a symphony of grace. Her gaze never left my features, savouring each change of expression with those soft liquid-dark eyes in which a hint of malice lurked.

'Will you please give me that letter?' I persisted, my annoyance increasing rapidly at her jeers.

'My dear Louise, I simply don't know what letter you're talking about!' Amusement flickered across her features, then: 'Who has been writing to you who shouldn't? George Fairman again? What has he been saying that you're afraid Gavin may see?'

I blinked in sudden surprise. Her mistaken belief that the letter had been written *to* me gave credence to her declaration that she did not know anything about it.

'No. It—' I paused, suddenly unsure of myself—'it was a letter *I'd* written to David Ross. I left it on the dressing-table so that I'd remember to post it when I next went out but it's—it's gone,' I finished weakly.

She gave a brief laugh. 'And you think *I* took it? Why should I do that, Louise? I'm not interested in your correspondence or your correspondents—although it sounds as if Gavin might be, doesn't it? Perhaps he wonders why you're so keen to keep in touch with your ex-boss . . . Did you have something going for you both in that direction?'

'I dislike your inference, Annabel,' I retorted icily. 'We were simply—'

'—good friends! Now where have I heard that before?'

'As you say, we were friends and I'm sure Gavin wouldn't stoop to removing my letters in order to censor them.'

'Why should you believe I would do such a thing?'

'There was mud from somebody's shoes on the carpet,' I answered, my reason sounding lame now in the face of her obvious determination to deny all knowledge of the missing letter. 'Someone went into the room after I left it.'

'And on the basis of that remarkable piece of Sherlock Holmes detection, you assume that *I* must be that particular person?' she asked.

'I think you'll admit you've shown an interest in my correspondence before,' I retorted.

'I assure you, Louise, that this time you haven't found the culprit responsible.'

Somehow I felt she was speaking the truth and the anger slowly faded as I muttered an ungracious apology for my own unforgivable intrusion into her room. I started to leave, embarrassed now that the wrath which had carried me on its crest had diminished.

'One moment, Louise.' Annabel spoke authoritatively and I turned in obedience to her command. 'I'd like a word with you, if I may, and I suppose that now ... while we're alone here ... is as good an opportunity as any.'

'A word with me? Why?'

I turned back to face her, suddenly unwilling to hear what she had to say but unable to think of an excuse to cut short this interlude which had, after all, originally been of my own seeking.

'I'd like to apologize for my outburst this afternoon,' she went on, after a brief pause. 'I felt a—a little surprised to hear you'd been to tea with Margaret. I couldn't understand why she should be so keen to get you to the cottage. I can only believe she's trying to cause trouble.'

'Trouble?'

'Oh, do sit down, Louise.' She cast an impatient glance towards the bed and, her tone irritated, she continued: 'You look the picture of outraged dignity standing there repeating everything I say like a parrot. What reason did Margaret give you to explain her motive for inviting you to Hope Cottage?'

Perching on the edge of the bed, I said: 'I've already told you. She wanted to assure me that Miranda's family no longer blamed Gavin for any part he played in the events which led to the fatal accident.'

She cast me a scornful glance. 'And did you accept that phoney excuse?'

I shrugged. 'I didn't know what to make of it all,' I admitted unwillingly.

'I'm not surprised. As she was the person responsible for causing all the unpleasantness for Gavin in the first place, it all sounds extremely odd to me.'

'She was responsible?'

'You're repeating my words again, Louise. I do wish you'd stop it.' She paused, then: 'She spread all the rumours around about Gavin. Did she mention *my* name at all?'

Momentarily uncomfortable, I took in a deep breath and replied: 'She said that you had deliberately turned away from your relatives in order to side with Gavin.'

Her lip twisted scornfully. 'No doubt for some devious reason of my own which would take little imagination to guess at.' Her eyes hardened. 'Margaret never changes. She's as cunning as she ever was beneath that sweet exterior. She doesn't have a heart . . . she has a lump of stone where it should be. She went to indescribable lengths to cause trouble here before, Louise. It seems to me that she's out to do the same thing all over again now that she's

117

managed to make contact with you. You're to be her next victim, I reckon. Watch your step!'

'But what trouble can she possibly cause me?' I protested. 'I shan't be visiting her again and I think she knows that now.'

'Don't underestimate Margaret Travers or Ed.' Annabel's face was thoughtful. 'Just be careful. We've all believed that we can't be touched by her malice but, nevertheless, all of us at some time have fallen foul of her. Philip was the scapegoat once when she wanted to cause trouble ... Then poor Gavin found himself at the centre of an official enquiry when he returned from a trip to the Far East and was greeted by the news of Miranda's accident ... Now *my* name is being torn to shreds ...' She sighed, her eyes momentarily saddened. 'I hope you won't take any notice of her scandalmongering, Louise. She's just a vindictive old lady who hasn't anything better to do than make mischief.'

'Don't worry, Annabel.' I got up, glancing at my wrist-watch. 'I shan't pay attention to her. I must go and change now or I'll be late for dinner.'

*   *   *

Gavin was sitting in our room, studying a sheaf of papers, when I returned. He looked up to regard me questioningly. 'Where have you been?'

I debated whether to tax him outright about my missing letter. Annabel's tiny seed of doubt had germinated and now I found myself wondering if Gavin himself were the culprit who had taken it. Could it be true that he had suspicions that my friendship with David Ross was not as innocent as he had once believed? Prudence won the day and I decided to wait for a few moments before mentioning the letter.

'I've been with Annabel,' I said. 'We were just talking.'

'I'm glad to see you two girls are getting on so much better now,' he responded. 'I noticed you both in the garden earlier and you certainly seemed to be interested in your topic of conversation. I always knew you'd hit it off if only you'd both give yourselves a chance to become acquainted.'

He returned his attention to the papers he had been studying and I smiled grimly to myself at his easy assumption of friendship between us. How like a man to believe what he wanted to believe! I did not fool myself that Annabel's dislike of me was any the less despite the fact that we had just imparted our confidences to each other.

'Mmm!' I said. Then crossing over to the dressing-table, I asked casually: 'Have you seen a letter addressed to David anywhere about, Gavin? I wrote to him and thought I put the envelope here but I can't see it now.'

He barely glanced up, his disinterest in the missing letter apparent. 'No. I've not seen it. You must have put it down somewhere else. I shouldn't worry about it. It'll turn up or, if not, somebody will be sure to post it for you.'

Annabel's theory of jealousy was mistaken. His complete indifference to the matter of my missing post would have convinced me for sure. I was also aware of a shaft of disappointment in the knowledge. Each day seemed to bring fresh evidence of Gavin's lessening feelings for me. I wondered how I was going to be able to bear it when he finally plucked up courage to tell me that our marriage had been folly on his part and he wanted his freedom. I knew I should not stand in his way or prevent him from leaving me if this was what he truly wanted. Even carrying the burden of love for him as I did, my pride would not allow me to try to hold him against his will. But the thought of a future without Gavin filled me with a cold sense of dread.

I was certain he was telling the truth. He had not seen my letter anywhere. I bit my lip anxiously as I wondered again about the identity of the person who had removed it from the dressing-table. It was not an important matter but I resented the inordinate amount of interest somebody was displaying in my affairs.

I also decided I should be well-advised to write another letter to David Ross and post it immediately since I was now all the more sure that my decision to spend a little time apart from Gavin was a wise one. David had offered me a temporary escape and I was determined to take it without any further hesitation.

CHAPTER THIRTEEN

It was not until three o'clock in the morning that I remembered something Annabel had said. A chance remark only and yet—

I could hardly wait for an hour which I deemed suitable to make another call at Hope Cottage.

As I made my way down the lane leading to the small stone house I found my thoughts circling around and around that casual sentence of Annabel's, wondering if I were reading too much into it. But it seemed to me that there were discrepancies which had to be checked. Though *why* I felt this way, I could not have said.

I walked up the narrow path leading to the front door; this time there was no sensation of unseen eyes watching my progress. The place seemed to be deserted, no sign of life apparent behind those closed windows. I rapped the door-knocker loudly, more self-confident today than I had felt yesterday. I knew now that the Travers—both mother and son—

boded no good intent towards Gavin and, my loyalty to him now uppermost, I was determined they should see my faith and trust in my husband were completely unshaken by their malicious tongues.

There was no response to my knock; all was still. I waited a few seconds and then repeated my efforts to obtain an answer.

Disconsolate as I accepted the fact that the Travers had made an early start about their business, I waited a moment on the step, then I started to move away down the path. Almost at the same moment the figure appeared from around the side of the cottage. We each paused, taken aback at our unexpected confrontation. Then the man moved towards me, an ingratiating smile upon lips too thin and tightly clamped to bear the gesture comfortably; there was obvious falsity in the friendly expression and I felt myself stiffen involuntarily.

'Morning,' he greeted me, as he approached. 'Been knocking long? I've been in the garden doing a bit of digging. Can I help you?'

'I—I'm wanting to see Mrs. Travers,' I explained. 'Is she in?'

'Mother's just slipped down to the village. She should be back shortly if you'd care to come in and wait.'

I already knew that this was Ed Travers and, instinctively, as when I had seen him in the wood, I distrusted him. I knew that I should have done so anyway without my private item of knowledge about his blackmail attempt on Gavin.

'If it wouldn't be a bother to you,' I said. 'I shan't take up much of her time.'

'Come on in.'

He took a key from his pocket and, opening the front door, led me to the room where Margaret Travers had entertained me the previous day. I had the impression even as I followed him into the place that he was somewhat put out of countenance by our unexpected encounter on the door-step. I remembered that I had hesitated a moment there, wondering whether to wait or return to Herren Towers and come back to the cottage later in the day. It was clear that Ed Travers had believed the caller had departed and was on his way to catch a glimpse of a retreating back. People do not usually dig gardens in shiny black leather shoes; neither do they manage to keep their hands as spotlessly clean as were his.

'Take a pew, miss. I don't think I caught your name.' He indicated the armchair I had occupied yesterday and I sat down in it. There was getting to be something repetitious about my visits to Hope Cottage, I decided wryly.

'Louise Summers,' I answered.

There was no change of expression on the thin, rather sly features. I knew that he was already aware of my identity and the question had been posed to bridge the momentary discomfort which existed between us.

'Oh, so *you're* Louise. Mother told me you'd called to take tea with her yesterday. I was out fishing.' A smile tilted the corner of his mouth. 'If I'd known her guest was to be *you* I'd have stayed to meet you then.'

'Really,' I acknowledged coolly, knowing that he lied and had been in the house throughout my visit the previous day.

'And to what do we owe the pleasure of another visit so swiftly?' he asked. 'Did you leave something behind? Mother didn't mention finding anything.'

'No. I just—just wanted to ask her something.' Obstinately I refused to divulge the precise reason for my presence; the light of curiosity which flickered in those light blue eyes was sufficient reward!

'And I can't help, Louise?' he prompted, after a brief pause while he waited hopefully for me to continue.

'No, Mr. Travers.'

He assumed a mock air of humility. 'Sorry, *Mrs. Summers*. I didn't realize that you regarded Miranda's kin as mere peasantry. I suppose the role of lady of the manor is still new enough to hold charms for you—not least being throwing your weight about in the village.' There was no secret now about the expression of enmity which tightened his features. 'If you feel so strongly about your position, I suggest you leave this cottage at once. It must be far too humble for the likes of you.'

I rose swiftly to my feet, angry but determined not to defend myself against those false accusations of his.

'Please tell your mother I called, Mr. Travers,' I said, turning sharply on my heels to leave this room, which was now filled with an atmosphere of smouldering anger. He stood, staring balefully after me, a brooding resentment shadowing his face.

Even as I reached the door, the sound of the front door opening heralded the arrival of Margaret Travers. She hesitated a moment as she saw me standing at the threshold of the sitting-room; glancing behind me, her eyes met Ed's with a question in their depths. Clearly she was aware of the unpleasant vibrations which made themselves felt about us.

'Louise, my dear! What an unexpected pleasure!' she said. 'I'm sorry I was out but I hope you've both introduced yourselves.'

'Oh, we've done that all right, Mother,' Ed returning, brushing past me and making his way towards the back of the house. Totally ignoring me, he met his mother's questioning gaze and added, as he went by her: '*Mrs. Summers* was just leaving but now you're back, I'll go instead.'

She regarded me in surprise as we went

125

back into the sitting-room together.

'You seem to have upset my son, Louise?'

'I just didn't care for his easy familiarity.'

I offered no further explanation and Margaret Travers did not press the subject.

'Would you like a cup of coffee?' she asked.

'No, thanks. I just wanted a word with you, if I may.'

She gestured towards the sofa and sat herself down in the nearby armchair.

'Go ahead, my dear. I suppose Gavin discovered you called here yesterday and threw a scene? I warned you he wouldn't like to know that we were so friendly.'

'Friendly?' I looked at her questioningly, surprising a look of malicious delight in her eyes.

'I would have hoped so after our agreeable little chat yesterday, Louise.'

'Why, during that agreeable little chat, did you lead me to believe that Gavin was responsible for Miranda's accident, Mrs. Travers?'

'Why? Because it's true, of course.'

'It's not—and couldn't be. You must know that. You were deliberately trying to make me believe the worst of him. Why?'

Her eyes narrowed. 'Why do you say such cruel things to me? I believed—' her face crumpled up like a child about to burst into tears—'believed we were going to be friends. I wanted you to know that we held no grievance

126

against Gavin for his carelessness.'

'There was no carelessness involved.'

'He removed the life-jackets, didn't he? Had they been in the boat Miranda might have been saved.'

'Gavin *couldn't* have removed them. And you know it.'

'He did—I tell you he did.'

'By remote control?'

Her face paled; there was a waxen appearance about her skin.

'I don't know what you're talking about. What are you trying to say?'

'Gavin couldn't have removed the life-jackets. He was away when Miranda took the boat out on the day of the accident. You told me a pack of lies! Why? Who are you shielding? Your son . . .? Annabel . . .?'

Fury made me spring to my feet. She cowered back as if afraid I should resort to physical violence. She had nothing to fear from me. Suddenly I wanted only to get away from her and her dreadful son.

'I didn't lie! Why didn't Gavin defend himself against the rumours? Answer me that, Louise Summers, answer me that!'

But I did not wait to hear more. I went with her words ringing in my ears, her question was one I had asked myself, over and over again. Who had he been shielding? It seemed to me there could be only one person. She who had resented my presence from my introduction into Herren Towers; she who made no secret of her dislike and jealousy of me.

Annabel. It had clearly been a slip of the guard she must keep on her lips when she had inadvertently let fall the information that Gavin had been away at the time of the accident.

Was *this* the knowledge which Ed held? The information which he held over Gavin's head in an attempt to gain money from him?

I felt sick with the secrets which had been thrust upon me.

I walked unseeingly out of the gate of Hope Cottage to collide with a tall figure who held me close in his arms, laughing down on me as I stumbled in shocked bewilderment after the impact.

'Hello, Louise. I've always longed for a beautiful woman to throw herself into my arms like that!'

'George! I—I'm sorry! I wasn't looking where I was going.'

My apology was faltering; I was suddenly filled with a need to unburden myself to this kindly man who had been a true friend to me since my arrival on the estate. But loyalty to Gavin stilled the urge.

'Just been visiting Hope Cottage, have you?' His glance was curious. 'Just like Daniel in the lion's den, eh?'

'What do you mean?'

He fell into step beside me as if sensing my

128

unwillingness to stand outside the Travers' cottage, feeling their eyes watching us from behind those curtains which shielded the windows.

'She's Trouble—with a capital T, Louise. Behind that sugary front there lurks a born troublemaker and her son is little better. I've already told you. He has an eye on the main chance and never loses an opportunity to make a quick buck.'

'He also has a chip on his shoulder the size of a house.'

George's lips quirked into a grin. 'Sounds as if you've already experienced a dose of Ed Travers for yourself. He's jealous as hell of Gavin—always has been.'

It was then that I began to put the jigsaw pieces into pattern. The personal disagreement between my husband and that man must have centred about Miranda. Was it possible that she had been having an affair with Ed? I could understand that Gavin with all his pride would never willingly stand for such a situation.

But—the question hit me again and again—would he have been capable of removing the life-jackets from Miranda's craft with the deliberate intention of causing her harm even if he had been in Cornwall at the time? I could not accept such an idea for a moment.

'Because—because of Miranda . . .?' I asked falteringly. 'Was Ed in love with her?'

George shrugged. 'Who knows? All one can say is that they were very close ... even for cousins.'

I felt my heart sink even lower. It was with an almost unbearable sense of loss that I was trying to come to terms with the knowledge that Gavin's love for Miranda might have been sufficient to cause him to—

But no! Relief surged through me as I remembered that Gavin had been absent at the time. George's next words, however, disturbed the fleeting reassurance I had gained by the thought.

'I imagine that you've heard the stories which circulated about Gavin at the time of the accident, Louise. Perhaps none of the mud would have stuck had it not been for the fact that he was seen in the vicinity of the boathouse a few hours before Miranda took the boat out. There was an eye-witness who was prepared to testify that he'd seen him leaving the place. Of course, he denied that he was there and his passport confirmed that he didn't arrive back in this country until the following day.'

'Then whoever saw him must have been mistaken, mustn't they?'

There was only the briefest pause before George spoke again, then his voice seemed to come unwillingly.

'But I wasn't mistaken, Louise. I know it was Gavin I saw on the beach that day.'

CHAPTER FOURTEEN

The rest of that walk back to Herren Towers passed as if in a dream. I wanted to pinch myself to make certain I was really there, really listening as George Fairman spoke those incredible words.

I knew that he apologized for telling me the truth; somehow the sense of it penetrated my fuddled understanding. But throughout the remainder of that nightmarish progress down the main drive, I felt as if I were being slowly torn to pieces somewhere deep inside me.

Had it been anybody other than George I should have scorned the tale as idle and mistaken gossip. But George Fairman was so reliable . . . so honest; he would never allow himself to make a mistake about a matter of such vital importance. I was also aware that he liked Gavin and would be unwilling to cause him more trouble without being very certain of his facts.

Aloud I told him: 'You must have been mistaken, George. Passport controls are too stringent to consider an error having been made there—quite apart from the fact that Gavin would be absolutely incapable of doing anything which would cause hurt to another.'

'He doesn't seem to have been doing too

bad a job with you,' he retorted sharply, catching me by the arm and wheeling me around to face him. 'Louise, get away from here while you can. Don't you understand that you're beginning to ask too many questions? You're raking over ashes that everybody had forgotten.'

'Everybody except you apparently.'

I pulled my arm from his restraining grasp and went to walk on. I had taken only a few paces when he caught me back once again, pulling me into his embrace.

'Did you think I wanted to tell you?' he demanded, his voice husky with suppressed emotion. 'Come away with me, Louise! Come away tonight! I love you and you can't pretend you're completely indifferent to me.'

Stunned, I paused there—too dumbfounded even to free myself from the circle of his hold. I had given him no cause to—It wasn't true! I could not have heard him correctly.

'Let me go, George!' My tone was cold, as cold as the chill which ran the length of my spine in that moment. 'I love my husband and I have no intention of coming away with you tonight or any night.'

His arms dropped to his sides; his face hardened as he realized how shocked I felt by his words. Then he shrugged, assuming an air of nonchalance which sat at odds with his earlier earnestness.

'All right! Please yourself! But don't come

running to me for help when Gavin decides he's had enough of marriage with you. And anybody can see the danger signals now, can't they?'

Taking to my heels I fled down the drive leading to the front door, his words ringing in my ears. He called something out after me but I did not hear it properly; I was deaf to everything except that last sentence of his which mocked me as if the words had taken on a physical substance of their own.

*   *   *

I got back to the house to be informed by Mrs. Harkness that Gavin had left a message for me. He had been called to London on urgent business and would be returning to Herren Towers the following afternoon.

The news came as a blow. It was only when the housekeeper relayed it to me that I realized how much I needed the reassurance which Gavin's presence would have given me.

George Fairman's words still haunted me and I knew I should not forget them until I felt Gavin's arms, strong and protective, about me.

Even his unexpected absence lent substance to the estate manager's cruel taunts.

I do not remember how I passed the rest of that day in detail. I have confused memories of helping Alice to arrange some flowers in the drawing-room; I seem to think I spent a period with Aunt Hettie who had recently been enjoying a more lucid spell; I wrote a few letters.

The family meal that evening seemed a ponderous and lengthy ordeal. I was thankful when, at last, I could plead an unaccountable weariness and retire to my room.

I was acutely conscious of Gavin's absence. I felt lonely and bereft of all support. Every fibre of my being longed for his presence in the room with me. I was also aware that if this brief example of a day in my life without Gavin were anything to go by, I should be hard pressed to manage the remainder of my life without him.

I could not forget George Fairman's cruel words with their suggestion that all was not above-board with Gavin's statement that he had been away at the time of Miranda's accident. But more disturbing even than this did I find his remarks concerning the state of my marriage with Gavin. Especially I could not forget that final barb of his: *'Don't come running to me for help when Gavin decides he's had enough of marriage with you. And anybody can see the danger signals now, can't they?'* The echo of those sentiments haunted me. I was unable to shake off the black cloud of despondency which gripped me.

Was the rift between us so obvious that even an outsider was able to observe it . . .? Where had the love gone which had once held us in such grip that I could not envisage anything having the power to mar that relationship?

I also found it incredible that George had been prepared to testify against Gavin at the inquest on Miranda's death. I had believed that he and Gavin were loyal friends and, in my book at least, friends did not betray each other—particularly in a matter as vital as this had been.

Sleep was an elusive bed-fellow. Question after question flitted through my troubled thoughts. Questions to which I could find no answers. The presence of Miranda in that lonely room with me was very strong. I had the impression that could I just pull back the misty curtain which separated us, I should see her standing before me in all her beauty. It was as if she wanted to tell me something—

I tried to shake off the mood which sat heavily on me in the lone watches of the night but I was relieved when at last I looked through the window and saw the first pale fingers of dawn light streaking the sky. Only then did I close my eyes and snatch a brief and restless oblivion from the troubles which beset me at this time.

*　　　*　　　*

The next morning a fine drizzle wiped out the view from the windows of Herren Towers: nevertheless, unable to rest indoors where the atmosphere weighed so oppressively upon me, I donned a heavy sou'wester and gum-boots and decided to take a brisk walk down to the cove. The path through the woods was like making my way through a long, dark tunnel; all was still, quiet—even the birds were silent in the trees around me. I hoped I should not run into George Fairman on my way to the shore and, for once, my wishes were granted.

Once in the cove I marched steadfastly into the rain in an attempt to shake off the gremlins which attacked me. The sea, with all its changing moods and faces, fascinated me and held me a willing captive; watching the waves froth and swirl around those treacherous rocks, the gulls wheeling vociferously overhead, I felt a sense of release from the anxieties which clouded my spirit. Only a few more hours now and Gavin would be home. I had already made up my mind to tackle him on the subject which obsessed me and now I tried to frame the words I would say. I wanted him to know I trusted him. *But, if I really trusted him*—whispered a tiny voice deep inside me—*would I be filled with this urgent need for his version of the events? Would I not be content to allow the sleeping dogs of the past to sleep quietly, undisturbed by probing questions and demands for explanations?*

'Hello, Louise! I wondered if I'd find you down here.'

Wheeling sharply, I turned to confront the

speaker, recognizing her voice immediately. Had she followed me from the house? I had seen no sign nor heard any giveaway footstep which might have revealed her presence. Perhaps the rain, which had now worsened considerably, had served to muffle the sound of her approach.

'Annabel! What on earth are you doing down here on a morning like this?' I smiled, adding: 'I always thought of you as a fair weather walker.'

There was no answering smile on her face as she fell into step beside me.

'Nothing would have dragged me out of doors on a day like this except that I thought we should have a talk, Louise.'

She gave a small shudder of distaste as a flurry of rain-drops suddenly hit her face and the playful wind tugged at the soaking head-scarf she wore. She looked drenched in her flimsy showerproof and I felt a moment's sympathy for her as she hopped over a small pool of sea-water which threatened to submerge her daintily shod foot. She was unsuitably dressed for walking in this inclement weather and my natural response was to urge her to return to the house at once.

'Then let's go back now,' I said. 'You're going to get soaked to the skin if you stay out in this much longer.'

'What I have to say is better said away from the house.'

I looked at her in surprise but her face was turned away from me, her expression unreadable.

'I can't imagine why. What can you have to say to me that necessitates all this cloak and dagger secrecy?' I spoke lightly but a warning prickle touched the back of my neck.

'You're interfering in matters which are none of your concern, Louise. You're making too many people search their memories about the events which happened on the day of Miranda's accident.'

'Why should it matter? Surely everything was brought out into the open during the inquest?' I tried to sound reasonable, calm, but my heart began to race as I wondered why Annabel considered it necessary to have this chat with me where it would be impossible for anyone to overhear what we had to say to each other. Strange, too, that her words should so nearly echo George's sentiments.

'I'm not here to answer your questions, Louise. I'm simply trying to warn you.'

'*Warn* me?' I echoed sharply. 'Why should I need to be warned?'

Her face was hard as she turned towards me, meeting my eyes levelly. There was a determination in the tight line of her mouth which I had never noticed before, a strength which made itself felt in that moment as our eyes met and held.

'You're making enemies—and sometimes

enemies can be dangerous.'

'Explain what you mean and don't talk in riddles to me.'

'You've been asking too many questions . . . seeing too many people who were deeply involved with Miranda and her life.'

I guessed that George Fairman must have told Annabel I had made another call at Hope Cottage. I wondered why he should have found it necessary to discuss it. Was everybody in league against me? *Or had Ed Travers told her?* Quick as a flash came the suspicion that the façade of dislike which the Travers had put up against Annabel might well conceal the fact that they were on friendlier terms than Gavin and the Summers family knew.

'Meaning Margaret Travers and her unprepossessing son?'

'Leave them out of it. You're just making your interest a little more obvious than is wise.'

'Why are you trying to stop me? What does it matter to you?'

'It's for your own good.'

'I don't think I believe you.'

'Then, Louise, you're a bigger fool than I took you for.' There was resignation in her tone now.

The rain was sheeting down harder, forming a curtain of grey water around us which merged into the greyness of the pewter-coloured sea. The pounding of the waves was loud in my ears, a regular pattern of sound like the heartbeats of the universe itself. I felt the tension mounting, increasing.

I paused in my steps, turning to look at Annabel. There was a threatening air about her and I took a step backwards; she thrust out a hand to catch me by the arm and I side-stepped, trying without avail to evade her grasp.

We were near the boathouse now and, unexpectedly, I caught a glimpse of Philip standing in the shelter of the doorway. I felt a wild surge of relief at the sight of him; like Providence itself he offered me a refuge from the enmity which surrounded me from this close proximity with Annabel on the lonely stretch of beach.

I had never before in my life been so conscious of the threat of danger; it was in the air about us, joining forces with the elements which combined to fill the atmosphere with a sense of menace and impending doom. The crashing of the waves on the shore echoed my own heartbeats now—no longer part of the outside world but a part of me—thrumming, beating, pounding with a force I'd never reckoned with before.

The glimpse of Philip standing there gave me a strength I had not known I possessed. He could not be seen now. He must have entered the boathouse to seek shelter from the torrential downpour. But the knowledge of his nearby presence afforded me the will to jerk my arm away from Annabel's restraining hand. I broke free and started to run in the direction of the boathouse, calling: 'Philip! Philip!' as I did so.

Like a distorted echo following me, I heard Annabel cry out: 'Louise! Wait! Wait for me! There are things you don't know!'

But her voice was lost on the wind, trailing away like the lonely cry of a seagull as fear lent my feet speed and the distance between us lengthened.

I felt rather than saw, her footsteps flag and pause before she relinquished the chase.

CHAPTER FIFTEEN

'Come inside, Louise. You must be soaked. What the devil possessed you to come walking by the shore on a morning like this?'

Philip drew me into the shelter of the boathouse, an arm protectively about me as he closed the door against the fierce onslaught of the downpour. I guessed he had not, through the heavy mistiness of the rain, seen Annabel who, failing in her intention to waylay me, had turned sharply on her heels in the direction of the cliff path which led to the woods beyond. I made no mention of her name to him. It was better that he did not speculate about the scene which his fortunate arrival on the spot had interrupted.

'I suppose I could ask you the same question!' I answered, relief flooding me as I realized I had reached a sanctuary where Annabel's animosity could not reach me.

The poor light from the high windows cast shadows around the building. All the accoutrements of the boathouse cluttered the surface of the floor and, straining my eyes against the gloom, I perceived the ropes and life-jackets stacked against the walls; an outboard motor: a small red sailing dinghy: a few fishing nets strewn carelessly over a pile of tea-chests. Incongruously, in the far corner there was a large settee, and it was towards this that Philip now led me.

'I?' He sounded momentarily taken aback, then: 'Oh, I just felt the need to get away from the house for a while. Where better than here?'

More accustomed now to the dimness my gaze turned towards his face, surprising an oddly wistful expression on his features. Carelessly he cast aside a pile of old newspapers from the settee and pushed me down into its capacious corner seat.

'There you are, Louise. Make yourself comfortable for a few minutes. We'll wait until the rain lets up a bit, shall we?'

He took the seat beside me, leaning back on his hands which he clasped behind his head. The rain thrummed steadily on the roof and the regular, insistent rhythm of it lent a soporific background to the musty, closed-up warmth of this unusual meeting-place. The smell of creosote mixed with oil vapours permeated the atmosphere in a strangely not unpleasant mixture.

I felt myself begin to relax now after those tense moments on the beach with Annabel.

The premonition of danger was still upon me, but I knew now the identity of my adversary and in that very knowledge found a certain comfort. Clearly Annabel hated me because I had taken Gavin from her in spite of all her scheming. Was this why she had resented Miranda? Because she loved Gavin ... desired to marry him herself? Had she removed the life-jackets from the boat and tampered with its engine with the deliberate intention of causing an accident when Miranda took the craft out? The idea seemed incredible—yet all the evidence pointed in its direction.

My wild thoughts ran riot until, with a start, I remembered that I was not alone. The realization that Philip was still sitting beside me in silent contemplation of my face brought me back to the present with a jerk; time enough for theorizing later when I could be alone to sort the puzzle into place. Suddenly I became conscious of the intensity of Philip's gaze and, as my eyes met his questioningly, his face relaxed into a smile.

'I was just thinking, Louise, that Gavin certainly knows how to pick 'em.'

I felt a fleeting embarrassment, swiftly displaced by surprise. There was a note in his voice which I could not fully explain but it jarred roughly on my ears. As I became aware of it, Philip moved closer to me, one arm encircling my shoulders. I tried to edge away, unwilling to give offence but not wishing to encourage this unexpected familiarity. His arm tightened, holding me firm. There was a wiry strength about him which was belied by the easy manner which characterized his casual approach.

'What's the matter, Louise? Afraid Gavin may find us here together and think the worst?'

His eyes sparkled gaily in the dim light. He was close enough now for me to feel his breath warm on my cheek.

I forced a light laugh.

'I hardly think Gavin has such a poor opinion of us both that he'd jump to conclusions like that.'

'Then it just shows how little you really know him, doesn't it, my poor, deluded little sister-in-law?'

'I think I know him very well,' I said levelly, 'but I do find this subject rather distasteful, Philip. Perhaps we could talk about something else?'

The smile on his face flickered only

144

infinitesimally. 'Yes, love. Let's talk about my dear brother's first wife for a change.'

'Is it still raining? Do you think we could go back to the house yet?'

I tried to get up from the seat as, pointedly, I shifted the conversation to another tack. Obstinately, Philip refused to be budged, pulling me back on the settee.

'No, not yet. We don't have much opportunity to talk, Louise—not alone.'

'I'm not aware that we have anything to say which makes the presence of other people redundant,' I said sharply.

'But that's just where you're wrong.' He reached out with his hand and twisted my face around to meet his taunting eyes. 'Wouldn't you like me to tell you about Miranda?' His voice was scarcely above a whisper now. 'I don't suppose Gavin's told you much, has he?'

'All that's necessary for me to know,' I snapped; a cold shiver lightly ran down my spine. 'I'm not very interested in Gavin's first marriage, Philip. It's the future that matters to me—not the past.'

'Brave words, Louise! Do you really mean them? If so, why are you going to Egypt without Gavin?'

I started in shocked surprise.

'Yes, I took that letter from your dressing-table,' he went on calmly. 'But never mind that now. It's Miranda I want to talk about. Can you honestly tell me you haven't wondered

145

about her ... wondered how much Gavin loved her ... wondered if he still misses her ... still thinks of her ...? If you're so disinterested in Gavin's past why have you taken the trouble to go to Hope Cottage and make yourself acquainted with the Travers?'

'How do you know I've been there?' I forced the words out through a throat gone suddenly dry; the atmosphere in this confined space was fraught with tension now.

'I followed you,' he answered simply.

'Why?'

He looked pained. 'Really, Louise! You ask foolish questions. I wanted to try to ascertain how friendly you were becoming with them.'

'Why should it matter to you? It was Gavin's name they were attempting to blacken—not yours.'

He smiled sneeringly. 'So there's still no love lost in that direction. Ed always was a fool who must take petty revenge over trifles. My guess is that he tried to blackmail Gavin ... probably he threatened to tell *you* the stories which circulated about Gavin at the time of the accident. When that ploy failed, Ed decided to drop a little poison in your innocent ear.'

It sounded a pretty accurate assessment of the situation to me, but I made no comment. Philip should receive no clues from me to appease his curiosity. I was keenly aware now of a need to escape from this wretched place, preferring to brave the elements and risk another encounter with Annabel rather than remain here with this man—who was displaying a side to his character I had not known he possessed.

The mixture of smells was cloying the air, becoming in an indefinable manner, more pungent, penetrating, and I was aware of a sense of nausea. I endeavoured to put mind over matter but the discomfort doggedly persisted—as did Philip's insidious voice with its malicious hints and suggestions.

'But you, I'm sure, Louise, still believe Gavin to be the innocent party, don't you?'

I didn't answer and he shook my shoulder as if in sudden irritation with me.

'Answer me, can't you?'

'Leave me alone! Have you taken leave of your senses, Philip?'

Once again I made a determined effort to get up, but again he pulled me back to the settee, less gently this time. I felt a slither of fear stir and snake through me before I regained control of my wayward emotions. How silly! As if my brother-in-law intended me any harm!

'Senses? I lost them when Gavin brought Miranda to Herren Towers, dear little sister-in-law. One sight of her and it was enough to drive any full-blooded man crazy with desire to possess her.'

Speechless with horror, I listened to Philip

with a sense of disbelief.

'And—you know what, Louise?—she wasn't above using that power of hers to attain her own ends, if it suited her book to do so.' There was a reflective expression on his face, as if, looking back into the past, he had for a moment forgotten my presence other than as a listener to words which seemed to be dragged from him by some force outside himself. 'One day she deliberately provoked Gavin into quarrelling with Ed over her and then made everybody believe that it was Gavin's jealousy which had caused the trouble. Ed . . . me . . . She played us off one against the other in order to spite Gavin.'

'To *spite* Gavin?' I echoed, my senses whirling.

'I thought she loved me,' he went on, almost as if he had not heard my interruption. 'I really believed she loved me. Then—just before the accident—she told me what a fool I'd been to believe she meant a word of all her promises. She'd never leave Gavin because *he* owned all this and she was determined that her child—*our* child, Louise!—was going to inherit Herren Towers and all that went with it.'

I sat listening in shocked horror as the meaning of his words infiltrated my bemused senses. Mixed with shock was the knowledge that Aunt Hettie had lied to me about Miranda's inability to bear Gavin the son he wanted. Oh, the tangled web of animosity, lies and deceit which had been spun here at Herren Towers! But at least this was not the reason Gavin had not asked Annabel to marry him as Aunt Hettie had wanted me to believe.

'*Your* child!' I heard myself whisper. 'You were unfaithful . . . with your own brother's *wife*! Philip! How could you have been so despicable!'

His lip curled into a sneer. 'Oh, Louise! You should just hear yourself!' He grinned derisively and went on, his tone mocking: '"Your own brother's *wife*" . . . Hasn't he told you? I find it hard to believe but, knowing Gavin, it's possible. Plays everything very close to his chest, doesn't he?'

I didn't answer and he continued: 'What you don't seem to know is that Gavin isn't my real brother. I was adopted by the Summers family . . . a foundling . . . of unknown parentage. Just a bastard . . . to be patronized by the Summers and brought up as their own.'

'And you repay their kindness with such a betrayal of Gavin's trust?'

'Betrayal! You don't know what you're talking about. *I* was the betrayed one . . . betrayed by Miranda. All her promises forgotten as if they'd never been made.'

There was a wild look in his eyes now and I felt an instinctive urge to run from this place and his presence.

'Now it's going to be my turn to get my

revenge . . . With *you* out of the way it will only leave Gavin . . . But *you* first, my lovely . . . so that he can suffer the hell that I've been through. Let him know what it's like to lose the only woman he ever cared about . . . as I did.'

My blood ran cold and a shiver moved swiftly down my spine. I had no need to ask him what he meant. Instinct provided the answer to the unspoken question. It was ironical that my flight from Annabel had brought me directly into the danger which I had tried to escape.

With a swift reflex action I tried to get up from the sofa. But with a speed swifter than mine, Philip's arm shot out, restraining me from making one move. He held me pinned in the corner of this seat we shared with such closeness I could feel the warmth of his body next to mine.

'Don't be a fool, Philip!' I snapped tersely, trying to sound braver than I actually felt. 'Let me go! It's time to stop playing games.'

'It's no game, sweetheart—not to me, it isn't. And I don't believe you'll consider it one either.'

'What—what are you going to do?'

His arm pressed even more tightly across me and I found it difficult to breathe against the constraining force of his hold.

'What do you think, Louise? I have plans for you—before I put you in that dinghy and take

150

you out to sea. My dear so-called "brother" has a gift for picking beautiful women. Are you as passionate as Miranda was, my darling?'

'You're mad!' I croaked. 'Mad.'

'I was never more sane. Everything's worked out according to my plans. I even guessed you'd take a walk along the cove this morning in spite of the rain. You're fond of walking alone brooding about Gavin, aren't you? Mind you, I admit I thought things had gone wrong when Annabel arrived on the scene. By the way, you seemed in a mighty hurry to get away from her. Why was that, Louise?'

'No reason. I—I—'

'No matter. There's no time for pettifogging small talk with you.'

I was aware that the tone of his voice had hardened, there was a cruel twist to his lips. I knew that he was actually enjoying this moment of power over me; he sensed my fear and the knowledge of it gave him a greater strength of purpose. I wanted to scream but, even as I opened my mouth to cry out, was conscious that no sound would come from my constricted throat.

Suddenly I saw how all my foolish fears and suppositions had been leading me in the wrong direction. I saw how false had been my various speculations, how wrong all my suspicions about Annabel. I wondered if Gavin had any idea that Philip was guilty of the—

I veered away from the direction in which

151

my thoughts were taking me, unwilling to give them credence by furnishing them with shape and form.

'You'll never get away with this, Philip!' The words were trite and I reminded myself of a star in a bad television movie. I went on: 'Let me go and I promise I'll never speak about this to a living soul.'

He only smiled and brought his face nearer to mine. I turned aside and, with a cruel grip, Philip held my chin and twisted my face back to meet his mocking regard.

'You'll certainly never tell a living soul, Louise. You see, the time has come when we must make an end to this play-acting. I've enjoyed this talk ... it's been good to speak about Miranda to somebody ... but time's running short.'

'Time?'

'"Time and tide wait for no man", don't they say? I want to catch the tide at its turn, Louise. We have to arrange our little accident, don't we? "Poor Gavin", they'll say, "how tragic that his second wife should have lost her life in a boating accident, too". Some ... the more malicious folk like Margaret and Ed Travers ... may even say he tired of you, too. But only you and I will know the truth, won't we, Louise? Only you and I ...'

CHAPTER SIXTEEN

I screamed. Philip's hand shot across my lips, stifling my call for help and, seizing my opportunity, I bit into the flesh with all the force I could muster. He let out an angry cry and, involuntarily, relaxed his grip for a split second. It was time enough for me to wriggle from his restraining hold and hurl myself up from the sofa and away from him.

But not far enough. How could I hope to out-distance Philip with his additional height and greater strength. He was hard on my heels as I ran across the boathouse floor towards the doors. My heart pounded madly; I was aware of sheer panic filling me with a sense of fear such as I had never before experienced. Arms flailing wildly I ran, knowing that my pursuer was almost on me and that I could not hope to escape him however hard I tried. But try I must if I had any wish to live.

They say that a drowning man sees his whole life flash before him in the last seconds before the sea claims him as its victim; I saw only Gavin's face and heard his voice, my whole being suffused with love for him and the longing for his presence. I heard myself scream his name aloud and the echo of it went on and on in my chaotic thoughts as if it were a call from the lips of a stranger.

I was almost at the doors—Mecca of all my

hopes—when my foot caught in the coil of rope flung carelessly on the floor. I tripped, crashing headlong to the ground, the breath knocked from my body in the impact of the fall. My dash for freedom could have taken only a few seconds and desperation now seized me as I realized my captor was almost upon me. Even as I struggled to get up, Philip's arms shot out, pinning me firmly to the ground.

I could see the hard and angry glint in his eyes as he brought his face closer to mine, his breath coming in harsh gasps which rasped in the sudden silence which now surrounded us. I struggled to move but it was hopeless pitting my puny force against him. Viciously he lifted an arm above his head and I caught the glimpse of steel clasped in his hand as he lunged towards me.

Again I screamed wildly as I fought to avoid the blow. But even as I did so I knew that I could not escape the lust for revenge which I had glimpsed in his eyes.

In the split second that his arm came towards me, I called once again for Gavin but his name faded on my lips as a crashing blow on the head knocked me into oblivion.

*   *   *

When next consciousness made me aware of the pain across my temples, I was afraid to open my eyes, fearing that I should still see Philip leaning over me with murderous intent in his face. I lost account of time as I listened, scarcely daring to breathe, for any tiny noise which might reveal his nearby presence.

Then it came. The sound of something being dragged across the boathouse floor. Through semiclosed eyelids I tried to make out what Philip was doing. I could just glimpse him pulling the dinghy down towards the doors; engaged in his task he spared no glance for my prone figure and I raised my head slightly in order to see a little better.

To my surprise I saw that he was wearing an old check coat of Gavin's, shabby though it was, its pattern was individual and unmistakable. Momentarily the fact that he had changed into this meant little. Then a sliver of horror passed through my body as the significance of it hit me with the physical force of a bludgeon. No wonder George Fairman had been prepared to testify that Gavin had been near the boathouse the day on which Miranda had met her fatal 'accident'. This was exactly what Philip intended anybody to think should they chance to gain a glimpse of him near the spot. Perhaps—and the thought sickened me—he actually *wanted* to be seen, his hatred for Gavin making him want to see my husband the scapegoat for his murderous intentions.

My thoughts were clearing as I became aware of my danger. I knew that I must act fast if I were to save myself from the fate which Philip planned for me. But I feared that any false move on my part would bring his unwelcome attention back to me and I remained still as I could while I tried to figure out what action I could possibly take.

Even as I debated the wisdom of making a run for it, Philip raised his head, glancing in my direction. Hastily I closed my eyes and, satisfied that I was still unconscious, he continued with his task of pulling the dingy nearer.

Once having dragged it to the position he wanted, he turned towards me and, advancing swiftly, lifted me bodily into his arms. I forced myself to remain limp and quiescent, despite my natural reaction to recoil from his touch. I steeled myself for the jarring crash I anticipated as he threw me into the dinghy, clamping my lips shut on any cry which might escape.

The sudden chaos which ensued as the boathouse doors were flung open from the outside filled all my senses, driving out all thoughts of fear in the hope that help was at last at hand.

Shouting. The sound of a shot being fired. Sobbing. The splintering of glass as it shattered.

All these impressions merged into one overpowering sensation of joy. I had recognized Gavin's voice as he called my name and, feebly, I tried to answer as I felt myself gathered into his arms.

Recognizing that I was safe at last, I clung to him, sobbing with a childlike need for comfort after the nightmare of the past minutes.

*   *   *

'How could I tell you, Louise?' said Gavin much later, in the privacy of our bedroom. 'How could I begin to tell you of the disillusionment . . . the love for Miranda which slowly changed into contempt . . .? It made me feel a failure . . . and when I recognized that barrier which was growing between us, too, I began to think that our love was going to follow the same pattern.'

I shook my head in an impatient gesture, moving closer into the protection of his encircling arms.

'It never could happen. I love you too much,' I protested.

'But not so much that you didn't decide to accept David's invitation to go out to Egypt?' he quizzed me lightly.

'How did you know about that?' I asked.

'How do you think? Philip lost no opportunity in telling me . . . insinuated that there must be an affair going on between you.'

Horrified, I gazed into Gavin's face. 'Did you—*do* you believe such a thing?' I demanded.

'Of course not. But I *did* begin to think you were having regrets about our own marriage. Perhaps after the fiasco of my life with Miranda I was all too ready to watch for the tiny pointers which might indicate that we, too, were heading for disaster.'

'I thought ... when you wouldn't discuss Miranda or your life together ... that I could never live up to her in your estimation. I began to believe you had married me on the rebound and now realized that—that you could never love me in the same way that you had loved her. You seemed to be so ... *distant*, so withdrawn ...'

'Because I was afraid of revealing my true feelings for you, Louise. I couldn't put into words the dread I felt at the idea of life without you ... for me it would have meant the end of everything I had held most dear.'

'Just think, Gavin!' I said, after a pause while I allowed the meaning of his words to sink in. 'Had it not been for Annabel's decision to fetch you down to the cove, then matters would have taken a very different turn.'

He buried his face in my hair, his words muffled as he replied: 'I never knew I'd have so much cause to be grateful to her. Thank God I'd completed my business and arrived home just after you'd gone out. I'd always considered her somewhat of a pain in the neck, to tell you the truth. She made her intentions to replace Miranda so obvious that I always felt I had to make an extra effort to be pleasant to conceal my real feelings.'

'But what alerted her to the danger this morning?'

'She caught a glimpse of Philip entering the boathouse and she saw that he was carrying an old coat of mine which has hung in the lobby for several years. She says that it was as if a missing jigsaw piece fell into place because she suddenly realized that it had been missing from the peg on the day of Miranda's accident.'

'I thought—I thought for a time . . . down there on the shore . . . that she was—'

He grinned ruefully as he cut in: 'Yes. She knows you did but she bears you no malice for the injustice. As a matter of fact, Louise, she told me this evening that she is considering returning to the States. She used to work on a radio station in New York,' he went on, 'and they've offered her a fresh contract which will provide her with her own chat show. She finds the idea attractive.'

I nodded, suddenly losing interest in Annabel now that she no longer provided any threat to my future happiness with Gavin.

'She'll stay here until after the case comes to Court. Philip will have to answer charges, of course.' He paused, then: 'I'm sorry, darling. We've an unpleasant time ahead of us with publicity.'

'We'll face it together,' I said confidently.

159

'That's all that matters, Gavin.'

He drew me closer, kissing me tenderly, the warmth of his body seeping into mine.

'I don't know what good thing I did to deserve you, Louise, but you more than compensate for the knowledge that Philip has secretly hated me all these years.'

There was an expression of sadness in his eyes which went straight to my heart.

'Why did he, Gavin?' I asked.

There was a moment's silence, then: 'Perhaps because he loved too much . . . loved Miranda as intensely as I love you.'

'No. I think it went even deeper than the fact that you were married to the woman he loved.'

I almost surprised myself with the sudden conviction that I was right. Gavin smiled, bestowing a kiss on my cheek.

'My wise Louise!' he teased gently. 'But I have to admit you're probably accurate in that assessment of the situation. Ever since Philip learned he was an adopted child, his jealousy has festered like a sore which wouldn't heal. God knows, perhaps the fault originally stemmed from my parents when they told him the truth about his background . . . His love for this house was as deep as my own—and yet he was suddenly stripped of all hope of ever possessing it . . . He fell in love with the woman I'd married and believed he was to be the father of her child . . . But even then she told him that she'd never surrender all that the Herren estates signified. Can't you imagine how bitter a blow it was to his self-esteem, Louise? Think how he must have determined to take his revenge on me . . . and how better than through *you*, my love!'

'But how could he have been so *wicked* as to try to set the blame against *you*?' I murmured.

'That would have been his final triumph,' he answered. 'When the set-up over Miranda failed to stick, he became even more embittered. He was determined that I should pay for being the legitimate heir of Herren Towers. If he'd only been a fraction more patient, I intended to—' He broke off.

'You intended to do what?' I prompted him.

'I was going to assign part of the Trust to him when came the time to settle the property on our son.'

I sat up in bed and looked at Gavin with wide eyes. 'Our son?' I echoed.

'That's what you want, too, isn't it?' he asked teasingly, pulling me back into his arms.

'Yes, but—'

'No buts,' he broke in firmly. 'We've already wasted too much time, Louise. It's as if our marriage has only just begun. The barriers are down between us. You belong to me and I belong to you until eternity, my love.'

There was a sudden urgency in his embrace and I clasped my arms about his neck, pulling him closer to me as if I would mould my body into his. His lips pressed down on mine with a bruising pain but I released myself just long enough to echo his words as if they were a promise to the future.

'Until eternity, my dearest love.'

We hope you have enjoyed this Large Print book. Other Chivers Press or G.K. Hall & Co. Large Print books are available at your library or directly from the publishers.

For more information about current and forthcoming titles, please call or write, without obligation, to:

Chivers Press Limited
Windsor Bridge Road
Bath BA2 3AX
England
Tel. (01225) 335336

OR

G.K. Hall & Co.
P.O. Box 159
Thorndike, Maine 04986
USA
Tel. (800) 223-2336

All our Large Print titles are designed for easy reading, and all our books are made to last.